CHAPTER ONE

SHE was going to be late.

Late. Late. Late.

The heels of Bella's shoes snapped out the word with every step, rebuking her, condemning her, telling her she would never measure up. She glanced at her watch and told herself to stop being absurd. She'd make the meeting exactly on time. She was being paranoid, that was all.

Still, she shouldn't have stopped to talk to Charlie. Or Emma. Or Sophie and Connor. She picked up her pace.

Failure. Failure. Failure.

What on earth had she been thinking?

Stupid. Stupid. Stupid.

She clenched a hand. Given what she'd overheard last week, she should've been more careful. She should've kept a closer eye on the time. She wanted to change her father's opinion of her, not reinforce it.

Spoiled, willful, doesn't have the sense of a goose! Bella doesn't know the meaning of the words 'dedication' and 'hard work'. That was what her father had said on the phone to her aunt in Italy last Wednesday. Bella had accidentally picked up the extension in the kitchen to ring out.

And it's my fault. She'd heard that before she could silently replace the receiver into its cradle.

She slowed to a halt, her throat constricting. The pain that had raked through her father's voice… She closed her eyes and rested her head against the wall. *Oh, Papa, I'm sorry.*

To know she'd disappointed him so badly, hurt him. Again. And to think he blamed himself.

She pushed away from the wall and straightened. She'd changed. The last eighteen months in Italy had seen to that. She would prove herself to him. She would make him proud of her.

As if to reassure herself, she rifled through the colour-coordinated folders she carried and then slapped a hand to her forehead. She'd left the sample menus in the canteen kitchen with Charlie!

She glanced at her watch and then tapped a foot. She could continue on to her father's office and be on time. Or she could race back down to the canteen, grab her menus and prove to her father and his right-hand man, Dominic Wright, how fabulously organised and creative she was and be a teensy bit late, which her father expected anyhow.

Organisation, creativity and proof of her dedication versus punctuality? Muttering an imprecation, she spun on her heel and sped back the way she'd come. Pulling in a breath, she started to jog. She rounded the corner, heard the faint 'ding' of the lift in the distance and broke into a run. She sprinted around the next corner…

'Hold the lift!'

But the lift doors closed before she could reach them. She pressed the button on the wall one time, five times, but the doors didn't open. The light above informed her that the lift had started its descent. She slapped a hand to the wall. Darn!

Pulling in a breath, she pushed her shoulders back. Okay, she could kiss her menus goodbye for the moment, but hopefully her colour-coordinated folders would at least give the impression of organisation and creativity.

She swallowed. As long as no one quizzed her too deeply about the contents of said folders. Katie, her father's secretary, had sent the main file through to her only last night with

A squeal from Bella alerted Dominic to an incoming rogue wave.

He grabbed her hand and hauled her out of its path, his arm going around her waist to half lift her. Breathless and laughing, she grinned up at him.

The breath shot out of him. His grip on her tightened. She stilled. He could read the question in her eyes—was he going to kiss her?

Would she let him?

When she didn't move away he had his answer.

Heat surged through him, the temptation pounding at him like the surf breaking on the reef. Bella would taste divine. He wanted to bury his face in her neck and inhale her, and then he wanted to capture her lips in his and devour her slowly, thoroughly. He wanted to memorise the curves of her body with his hands. He—

Icy water hitting his feet and ankles brought him back to earth and made Bella jump, breaking the spell.

BELLA'S
IMPOSSIBLE BOSS

BY
MICHELLE DOUGLAS

First published in Great Britain 2012
by Mills & Boon, an imprint of Harlequin (UK) Limited.
Harlequin (UK) Limited, Eton House, 18-24 Paradise Road,
Richmond, Surrey TW9 1SR

© Michelle Douglas 2012

ISBN: 978 0 263 22795 6

Harlequin (UK) policy is to use papers that are natural, renewable
and recyclable products and made from wood grown in sustainable
forests. The logging and manufacturing process conform to the
legal environmental regulations of the country of origin.

Printed and bound in Great Britain
by CPI Antony Rowe, Chippenham, Wiltshire

At the age of eight **Michelle Douglas** was asked what she wanted to be when she grew up. She answered, 'A writer.' Years later she read an article about romance writing and thought, *Ooh, that'll be fun.* She was right. When she's not writing she can usually be found with her nose buried in a book. She is currently enrolled in an English Masters programme for the sole purpose of indulging her reading and writing habits further. She lives in a leafy suburb of Newcastle, on Australia's east coast, with her own romantic hero—husband Greg, who is the inspiration behind all her happy endings. Michelle would love you to visit her at her website: www.michelle-douglas.com

Books by Michelle Douglas:

THE MAN WHO SAW HER BEAUTY
THE SECRETARY'S SECRET
CHRISTMAS AT CANDLEBARK FARM
THE CATTLEMAN, THE BABY AND ME

To Annie,
for all the coffees, caramel doughnuts and Black Russians.
Thank you!

a pleading, *For all you hold sacred, please don't tell your father how late I am on this!* Bella hadn't had time to do more than print the file off. She'd reserved this afternoon for poring over its contents.

She glanced at her watch. If she put her skates on, she wouldn't be late to the meeting after all.

She put her skates on.

Professional, she lectured as she sped down the corridor. Chin up, shoulders back. She had to exude confidence and competence. Especially competence. She had to prove to her father that his faith in her wasn't misplaced.

If he actually had any faith left in her.

She pulled in a giant breath as she was ushered into her father's office. She took one look at him and had to fight the urge to rush across and kiss his cheek, to envelop him in a hug and tell him how much she loved him and how much she had missed him while she'd been in Italy.

Professional. She had to be professional. Kissing him, hugging him, would not earn her his respect. Especially as he wasn't alone. She gripped her folders more tightly and resisted the superstitious urge to cross her fingers. She didn't need superstition. She needed a chance to prove herself, that was all.

Marcello Luciano Maldini turned to her. 'You're late!' he snapped.

She glanced at her watch and raised an eyebrow.

He glanced at his watch and scowled.

Oh, how she wished he would smile!

He didn't smile. She did. She was so glad to see him. She was so glad to be here. She was so grateful to him for this opportunity. She did her best to not make the smile too broad, though. She did her best to make it professional and polite. 'Good morning, Papa. If I am late, then I am most sincerely sorry.'

He blinked and for a moment she thought he might apologise for his gruffness, perhaps even admit that she hadn't been late.

He didn't. He folded his arms and glared. 'My secretary rang your mobile phone and left a message informing you that the meeting was to be brought forward fifteen minutes.'

She *was* late! And all because she'd turned off her phone so it couldn't distract her from the most important meeting of her life.

She gripped her folders so tightly she broke a nail. 'I'm sorry. I turned it off so it wouldn't disturb my preparations for our meeting.'

Her father huffed out something she didn't quite catch and turned away. All her old fears surfaced: *Failure. Stupid. Fool.* She did her best to beat them back.

'Dominic, I would like you to meet my daughter, Bella Maldini. Bella, this is Dominic Wright.'

As the man turned towards her, she opened her mouth to say, 'Pleased to meet you,' but the moment her eyes collided with the Mediterranean blue of his, the words evaporated.

Dear Lord. Blue eyes shouldn't make a girl speechless.

Nor should red hair.

But the combination…

She tried to expel the air held prisoner in her lungs. She hadn't believed Catriona and Cecily when they'd said he was gorgeous *and* that he had red hair—tawny, red-gold, like a lion's mane.

Don't gape. Don't gape. Professional!

She cleared her throat. 'I'm, um… Pleased to meet you, Mr Wright.' Her voice emerged high and strained, breathy. She bit back a groan. Where was professional?

'Dominic,' he corrected.

This was the man who held her entire future in his hands? Her white business shirt tightened around her ribs, constricting her breathing further. According to her cousins, Dominic—with his looks and his charm—was the most dangerous man in Sydney. Break-your-heart dangerous. They'd said he'd eat a little virgin like her for breakfast.

All silly, teasing nonsense, of course.

To be honest, he looked more like 'scary boss' material than the playboy Cat and Cecily had reported, and he was eyeing her up and down right now with those mesmerising eyes as if he could sum her up in all of ten seconds. As if she only had ten-second's worth of value to sum up.

He didn't say he was pleased to meet her. He didn't smile.

With a super-human effort, she kept her smile in place. 'For form's sake, you're supposed to say that you're pleased to meet me, too, Dominic.'

His grin when it came was slow and crooked. It hitched up the right side of his mouth. The creases around his eyes deepened. The blue of his eyes intensified. 'I'm pleased to meet you, Bella.'

Just for a moment the room receded, and then with a roar it came rushing back. Uh-huh. So her cousins had been right, then.

Playboy—tick.

Heavenly, golden, gorgeous—tick, tick, tick.

Temptation personified—tick.

When Dominic held out his hand, she took it automatically. She couldn't manage a single solitary syllable. His hand curved around hers and he simply held it.

Her pulse throbbed.

'Delighted,' he murmured.

She found her voice. 'Absolutely.'

She tugged her hand free and went back to clutching her folders, did what she could to ignore the tingling that the palm-on-palm contact had triggered against her bare skin. For all his tawny goldenness and the warmth of his smile, he was known as The Iceman. *And don't you forget it!*

It didn't change the fact that he was the one man who could sway her father's opinion. She would have to tread carefully.

'If you've finished sizing each other up,' her father said

brusquely, 'can we sit and get this meeting underway? Come—sit, sit.' He shooed them to their seats.

From beside her, Dominic's heat beat at her. She kept her eyes on her father. *Professional.*

Marco steepled his hands on his desk. 'Dominic, I want you and Bella to work on the Newcastle Maldini,' he said without further ado. 'I want the pair of you to have it ready for the grand opening in eight weeks' time.'

Triumph surged through Dominic. Years of training, though, ensured he didn't betray that triumph by so much as a flicker of an eyelid. Taking charge of Marco's flagship hotel was the first step in taking over sole management of the Maldini Corporation's fledgling tourism arm. If the Newcastle Maldini proved a success, then plans for expansion would forge ahead—a chain of five-star Maldini hotels in all the major cities in Australia. After that, the international market—New York, London and Rome. The possibilities multiplied with exciting potential.

He'd wanted a change, needed it. Two and a half months ago he'd made his position clear to Marco—either a sideways move within the Maldini Corporation or he'd look elsewhere. Heading up the corporation's tourism operations fitted the bill exactly. Marco had delivered on his promise and Dominic had every intention of ensuring the Newcastle Maldini not only met but exceeded Marco's expectations.

He hadn't counted on getting foisted with the boss's daughter, though.

He glanced across at her and his gut tightened. She looked nothing like the plump, dark-haired child from the photograph that sat in pride of place on Marco's desk. She looked nothing like the woman he'd imagined as he'd sat across from Marco at this very desk countless times in the past six years and listened as the older man had despaired of her. 'You want Bella to work on the hotel?' He didn't try to hide his disbelief and scepticism.

Bella stiffened. Then she leaned towards her father. 'You haven't told Dominic about your plans for us to work together before today?' Her mouth opened and then closed. She swallowed. 'But you made that decision last week.'

Marco slapped a hand down on his desk. 'I do things my way, young lady. This is my office and in my office my word is law.' He stabbed a finger at her. 'I'll run my company the way I see fit!'

She sat back. 'You didn't tell him because you thought he'd refuse to work with me.'

Marco's jaw worked but he didn't say anything. He didn't have to. To himself, Dominic acknowledged the truth of her accusation. If he'd known about this a week ago, even two days ago, he'd have constructed every argument available against it. And Marco would've given way. Marco didn't want to lose him.

He cleared his throat. 'Marco, exactly what role do you envisage for Bella at the hotel?'

His employer heaved out a sigh, lifted a hand and let it drop. 'Bella tells me she can create the restaurant of my dreams. Her expertise will be confined to the kitchens and dining rooms. You, of course, will be in charge of operations.'

He nodded. He hadn't expected anything less.

'And you, my girl—' he turned to Bella '—will consult Dominic about everything.'

'Of course.'

Dominic wasn't fooled for a moment. Behind that lush mouth and those caramel melt-a-man-to-his-seat eyes, Bella was fickle, capricious and unreliable. Marco had given her countless opportunities to establish herself in a profession, but she had squandered all of them. Her seeming compliance was merely a pleasing façade for Daddy's benefit. She might fool Marco, but Dominic had no intention of falling under the spell of that butter-wouldn't-melt smile. He was not his father's son.

'She knows nothing about management styles or systems,' Marco warned him. 'All she knows is cooking and kitchens, so you'll need to show her the ropes.'

Marco had to be joking, right? Bella wouldn't stick to this job any longer than she'd stuck to anything else. Marco might be prepared to waste his time and expertise on someone who wouldn't appreciate it, but Dominic had no intention of doing so.

He stared at Bella. She met his gaze unflinchingly. He glanced across at Marco, who gazed at Bella with all the love in his generous heart on display and something inside him started to ache. There weren't too many people Dominic could claim to love, but Marco was one of them. His jaw tightened. He forced it to relax. For Marco's sake, he owed Bella the benefit of the doubt, at least for the duration of this meeting. 'Okay.' He nodded. 'You think Bella has something of value to offer the hotel?'

Marco straightened. 'Bella,' he clipped out. 'Show us those menus you told me you've been slaving over. You said you'd have samples ready for today.'

She hesitated. 'There's a slight hitch with that, I'm afraid.' She crossed her legs and smoothed out her skirt with an aplomb that almost stole Dominic's breath. 'I've left the menus in the canteen kitchen. I was discussing them with Charlie earlier.'

There was an awkward pause. Dominic schooled his lip not to curl. He doubted the existence of any such menus. The way Marco studiously avoided meeting his eyes told him Marco thought them products of Bella's imagination, too.

'I can run down to the canteen now and retrieve them, if you like. Or I can outline them to you verbally.'

While he was tempted to call her bluff, Dominic didn't want her compounding lie with lie. He didn't approve of her, but he didn't want to embarrass Marco either. Marco deserved better than that.

He cleared his throat. Both Bella and Marco turned to him.

'Why don't we leave the menus for another day? There's plenty of time.' He nodded to the folders Bella held in her lap. 'Why don't you tell us what you've brought along instead?' He hoped she had something there that would make Marco proud.

Her tongue snaked out to moisten her lips. Her fingers curled around the folders until her knuckles whitened. Dominic leaned back. The pampered princess didn't have quite as much aplomb as he'd thought. She was nervous. Maybe he'd done her an injustice. Maybe this meant a lot to her.

'The folders, Bella,' he said gently. In his experience, folders meant show and tell. She wouldn't have brought them along if they didn't contain something that would show her off to good effect. He'd give her every chance to show off if it'd make Marco happy.

'These aren't anything particularly interesting.'

He didn't trust that shrug. It was too studied.

'These are simply the files my father sent me about the hotel, along with some information I've started to gather about Newcastle.'

She really had nothing? Did she seriously mean to take such blatant advantage of Marco?

'I take it you've read the information your father sent you?'

'Of course.' But she didn't meet his eye as she said it.

He crossed his leg and hoped it hid the sudden fury that coursed through him. 'Off the top of your head can you tell me the number of staff you will have working under you in the restaurant?'

She moistened her lips. Again. He wanted to feel a savage triumph that he could succeed so easily in unsettling her. Only he was the one who was unsettled—by the beguiling fullness of her bottom lip, the shine there that beckoned to him.

'I'm afraid I can't remember that off the top of my head. I've only had a chance to scan the documents.'

He allowed his lip to curl a fraction. 'I see.' If Marco had made the decision about the hotel a week ago, Bella would've had the documents a week ago. He knew Marco.

She swallowed. A faint pink tinged her cheek. Dominic bit back something rude and succinct. 'Then can you tell me what interesting pieces of information you've gleaned about Newcastle in the course of your research?'

Panic raced across her face. 'I, uh… It's the second largest city in New South Wales. It's a coal port and…and its former prosperity came from its large steel works. And, um…' She blinked rapidly. 'And it's known for the beauty of its beaches.'

'So, in fact, you have nothing more than a general knowledge of the place?'

Her chin shot up at that. 'I'm working on it.'

Her eyes did strange things to his insides. He hardened his heart. It'd be better for her to disappoint Marco now rather than later on. 'Can I see your folders?'

'Why?'

'Indulge me.'

She glanced at Marco as if hoping he'd step in, but to Marco's credit he remained silent. With obvious reluctance, she handed them over.

He flicked through the contents of the top folder. As she'd said, it held the information about the hotel. The printed sheets were so tidy it was obvious that they had yet to be disturbed by human hands. He shook his head. No wonder she couldn't recall staffing numbers; she hadn't read them to begin with.

The second folder held print-outs, clippings and brochures about Newcastle. At least she hadn't been lying about that.

The last one…

'That's personal. I—'

He pulled out a lingerie catalogue. A lingerie catalogue! He smothered an oath. Marco had to see that Bella just wouldn't make the grade on this one.

She snatched the catalogue from his hand. 'A friend has a

party-plan company. She asked me to take a look. I had nowhere else to put it.'

He didn't doubt which reading material she preferred. He handed the folders back.

He found himself combatting a sudden weariness; a feeling of lethargy and emptiness. He tried to shake it off. 'What qualifications do you have, Bella?'

Her eyes flashed fire. 'If my father has no qualms in that area, then I don't see what concern it is of yours.'

'It's my concern because I'm going to be ultimately responsible for the hotel's success. Marco?'

Marco raised a hand and then let it drop. From beside him, he felt Bella flinch. It took all his self-control not to turn back to her.

'For the last eighteen months my daughter has been working in her uncle's restaurant.'

'Were you in charge of its day-to-day management?'

'On occasion.'

He shook his head and turned back to Marco. 'This is never going to work. Bella simply doesn't have the experience necessary for such a senior position.'

'She'll be able to pull it off with your help.'

He wanted to turn away from the pleading in Marco's eyes. He owed the older man a lot, but to be party to Bella's latest whim? A whim that no doubt would end in Marco's disappointment and regret. He pinched the bridge of his nose between thumb and forefinger.

'Maybe you're right,' Marco said. A sigh heaved out of him. 'Maybe this is nothing more than an old man's dream.'

Dominic glanced up. Before his eyes, Marco seemed to age.

'No!'

Bella leapt to her feet. Dominic couldn't do this to her. He couldn't!

Her hands clenched about the folders. She stared at her father. That expression on his face! It reminded her of the time he'd seen her high school graduation results. 'No Maldini has ever failed high school!' Oh, that look—it had cut her to the quick. He hadn't said anything else. He'd turned away. He'd cancelled what was supposed to have been a celebratory dinner. He'd gone out alone.

She couldn't let him turn away now.

'Don't listen to Dominic.' She slammed her folders down on his desk. 'On paper I may not have the qualifications, but I have the heart and I have the talent.' She prayed she had the talent.

She glared at Dominic. 'How do you rate determination and talent, Dominic?'

He stared up at her. He hadn't moved. Her heart pounded; she swore both he and her father must hear it.

'Highly.'

She could tell he didn't believe it, but…

'I have both. In quantities that I promise will impress even you.'

He didn't reply. She glanced at her father and her stomach tightened when she recalled the way his face had frozen when she'd confessed that she'd dropped out of university. He'd barely been able to look at her. It had made something inside her curl up and die.

That wasn't going to happen now. She wouldn't let it.

She swung back to Dominic. 'Before she died, my mother's dearest wish was that my father would one day create the hotel of his dreams. It was a dream close to both their hearts. It is a dream close to my heart. Papa—' she swung to him '—you know this is true.'

It was the reason she'd badgered him to give her the opportunity to work at the Newcastle Maldini. She'd begged, pleaded and cajoled until he'd agreed. Dominic was not going to take that away from her.

She pulled in a deep breath. Before Italy she'd have agreed with Dominic's assessment of her. Before Italy she'd never have dared take a risk like this. But her experiences in Italy had changed her. She'd found her passion. She'd found a talent—something she was good at. She'd discovered what she wanted to do with the rest of her life. She believed she had something to offer. Something good and true.

She trembled as she played her trump card. 'Papa, Mama would want you to give me this chance.'

As she'd known it would, the mention of her mother defeated him. His shoulders sagged, he sighed and stared at Dominic. 'It was my Francine's fondest wish…'

It took all her courage to meet Dominic's gaze. Would he back down? Would he relent and give her a chance to prove herself? His eyes were unreadable. His face could've been chiselled from stone, or ice.

'You think you are up for this?' he finally said, the soft threat of his voice sending a shiver of apprehension up her spine.

'Yes.' Somehow she made her voice strong.

He glanced at her father and just for a moment his expression softened. It hardened again when he glanced back at her. 'You will work hard?'

That sounded less a question and more of a threat. She swallowed. 'Yes.'

She refused to let her gaze drop from his, but she still didn't have a clue what he was thinking. But those eyes, the bluest of blue, brought to mind hot, languid days on the Mediterranean… and hot, languid nights. Heat flowed into her cheeks, her neck, her breasts.

Very slowly, Dominic gave a smile. She didn't know what that meant either. It wasn't the kind of smile she'd ever been sent before. Without taking his eyes from her, he addressed her father. 'Perhaps, Marco, Bella deserves your confidence? The final decision rests with you.'

'You will work with my Bella?'

Dominic blinked and released her. She found herself breathing hard. For a moment she wasn't sure where to look.

'I will work with Bella if that's truly what you want.'

Her father literally beamed at Dominic. It made her heart burn. Dominic received the beaming smiles for making the sacrifice to work with her, while she...?

'And as long as Bella is sure that's what she wants, too.'

The same soft threat threaded his words. Marco glared at her. She lifted her chin to hide her hurt. 'Of course it's what I want.'

Marco dusted off his hands. 'There, that's settled then.'

She swallowed. She would deserve those smiles soon, too, she swore silently. Her father would be proud of her. As long as she didn't screw up.

Please, God. Don't let me screw up.

CHAPTER TWO

DOMINIC sat ramrod straight and tried to find his equilibrium as Bella resumed her seat and proceeded to outline her plans for the restaurant and the type of cuisine she wanted to serve. Something about the woman rocked his balance. He searched for righteous anger, for indignation and scorn, but that comfort eluded him, too.

It didn't mean he advocated her tactics. He loathed those. She'd emotionally blackmailed Marco into giving her the job, and yet...

The fire in her eyes when she'd leapt to her feet. The utter life that thrummed through her. It had burst from her as if her body couldn't contain it.

He'd seen it, and for a moment it had turned everything upside down.

He'd demanded a sideways move within the Maldini Corporation for one reason alone—he hoped the new challenge would help drive away the emptiness that had started creeping over him in the last few months, the boredom and *ennui*.

He glanced at Bella again. Even under the polite cover of professionalism she'd now assumed, he could sense the fire in her, simmering just below the surface. He didn't know what name to give it—zest, freedom, vitality? He had a feeling that if he could identify precisely what it was he'd find the answer to the emptiness that yawned through him when he least expected it. The emptiness that sucked all enjoyment out of life and left him feeling grey...blank. Emptiness he found harder and harder to fight each time it descended. Emptiness that had no reason for being. If he studied her, he might find the answer.

He took in her pouting lips and the long, dark fall of her hair as she listened to something her father said and his skin tightened. She crossed her legs and her skirt rode up, exposing a long length of tanned thigh. Heat arrowed into his groin and his senses suddenly blazed to life. Colours became instantly richer and he found himself appreciating the deep garnet-red of her suit, relishing the way it outlined her lush curves and highlighted the thick darkness of her hair. Smells sharpened until he could practically taste the lemon tang of her scent.

He bit back a curse. It had been a long time since a woman had fired him with such an instant response. Why Bella? Why now? He didn't lack for female company—beautiful female company—and he'd made no secret of the fact that he liked women and that he liked variety in women. If Bella had been anyone else...

If she'd been anyone else he'd have sworn to have her in his bed by the end of the week.

He couldn't. She was Marco's daughter, for God's sake.

And for the next two months he would have to find a way to work with her.

He stared at her folders, now sitting innocently on Marco's desk, and his lips twisted. A blasted lingerie catalogue! He considered how shamelessly she'd just played her father. He thought back to all the women who had coldly taken advantage of his father and a seam of ice threaded through his veins. Bella wouldn't find him so easy to manipulate.

It didn't mean he couldn't play her at her own game. She would not let Marco down this time. Dominic wouldn't allow it. This time his reputation was on the line too and, if he had to charm her into compliance, he would.

Bella turned to him. 'What do you say, Dominic?'

He hadn't followed the conversation at all. No matter. He

raised one shoulder in as languid a shrug as he could manage. 'I'd say it's going to be quite an experience working with you, Bella. I respect your—' he let his gaze drop to her lips '—enthusiasm.'

'I… Thank you.'

Rather than reach across and shake her as he itched to do, he sent her his trademark smile instead. The effect was devastating, or so he'd been told. He didn't consider himself vain but he wasn't falsely modest either. That smile had brought enough women to their knees for him to believe in it.

Bella's eyes narrowed to thin pinpricks of hauteur. She looked as if she'd rather slap him than fall to her knees. It'd take more than a smile to knock this lady off her feet.

Unfortunately, that only made his interest level shoot up several notches. 'I want to make it clear that I won't make concessions for you because you're Marco's daughter.' He personally meant to ensure that she worked her butt off.

She tossed her head. 'I wouldn't expect you to.'

'I demand excellence.'

Her chin tilted at an angle that had him dying to kiss her. 'I'm glad to hear it.'

He would make her toe the line and see this project through to its bitter end. She'd make good on her promise to Marco this time. He'd see to that. This time, when the going got tough and she tried to bail—and he'd make sure it got tough—she'd find his will more implacable than her own.

Bella was going to get exactly what was coming to her.

CHAPTER THREE

BELLA tried to smile at the cat, but it glared at her through the bars of its cage as if it knew she didn't really mean it. It hissed when she readjusted the holdall over her shoulder. It spat when she dropped the other bag to the floor.

'You might be a pedigree chocolate-banded Abyssinian, but you're still just a cat, you know,' she muttered under her breath. 'In a cage,' she added for good measure.

She fumbled with the door key and tried to keep the cage as still as possible. From the noise Minky was making, you'd think Bella had seized the cage in both hands and was shaking the life out of it.

She finally managed to get key in keyhole and started to turn it at the precise moment the door flew open and practically wrenched her arm from its socket. The momentum flung her inwards. Before she knew which way was up, she found her face mashed against hot male flesh.

Dominic's hot male flesh.

The hot male flesh of Dominic's *naked* chest.

For a moment everything froze. Him. Her. Time. Even Minky. But not for long. The cat hissed again, time sped back up and Bella forced herself to plant a hand in the middle of Dominic's *naked* chest and push herself upright.

Only then did the full impact of his semi-nakedness slam into her. Oh, dear Lord, Dominic looked like some golden devil sent to tempt all of womankind. Her knees actually weakened.

Broad, muscular shoulders angled down a powerful chest to a stomach a woman could crack walnuts on, and then down farther to lean hips encased in a pair of low-slung jeans. Heat flushed through her. Her, 'What the hell are you doing in my apartment?' got choked up in the back of her throat, making her sound as if she had a fur ball.

Perspiration beaded her top lip. The spattering of light hair on his chest, its crispness still imprinted against her cheek, tapered down to his navel and disappeared beneath the waistband of his jeans. Perspiration trickled between her breasts and down her spine, making her shirt cling to her back.

'Oops?' he offered when she remained silent.

He looked disgustingly cool and unfazed. It made her aware of how crumpled and unkempt she was. She scowled. Dealing with Dominic at the office promised to be enough of a challenge let alone outside of it. Her apartment, she'd already decided, was going to be a strictly no-Dominic zone.

She hitched up her chin and tried to keep her eyes above shoulder level. 'What, may I ask, are you doing in my apartment?'

'Ah... There's been a hiccup on that front.'

Great.

'Apparently only one apartment was booked.'

She let the holdall slide from her shoulder to the floor. She set Minky's cage down next to it and dusted off her hands. 'Then I'll go and talk to the apartment manager and organise another one.'

'I've already tried that.'

She'd started to turn away. She turned back at his words. Her skin prickled with foreboding. 'And?'

'And there isn't another apartment available in this block for another seven weeks. In fact, there isn't another apartment to be had in the whole of Newcastle for the next eight days. Three affiliated events are taking place here this week—a literary festival, an art festival and a youth-culture festival, along with

some associated popular-culture conference. The only accommodation available involves a tent.'

He had to be joking! She gaped at him.

'Chin up, Bella. This is a penthouse apartment. It's huge.
There's more than enough room for the both of us.'

It didn't matter how big it was. It wouldn't be big enough
to…

'Look, I know it's not ideal, but this is business, Bella. You
either roll with the punches or you get out.'

Get out? No way! She wasn't leaving. Dominic might not
want her on his team but he wasn't getting rid of her that easily. She pursed her lips and resisted kicking the bag at her feet.
'The apartment is large, you say?'

'Huge.'

'How many bedrooms?'

'Two.'

She glared at him. *Eyes above shoulder level.* 'This means
setting some house rules.'

He raised both hands in the air. 'Whatever.'

She yanked the holdall back to her shoulder and picked up
Minky's cage. *House rule number one: no naked men!*

He reached out a hand towards her and she tensed until she
realised he only meant to take the holdall from her shoulder. He
picked up the bag at her feet and led the way into the apartment.

Bella followed him then stopped dead and gaped. She
choked. 'Oh, my God!'

'Yep.'

She dumped Minky unceremoniously on the coffee table
and swung in a slow circle. Dominic had obviously done his
best, opening the heavy velvet drapes as wide as they'd go,
encouraging light to spill into the room, but the burgundy-
coloured carpet seemed to absorb the light to create a strange
pink glow.

'What is this?' She didn't even try to camouflage her horror.

'My initial reaction is to say, ghastly.'

She almost grinned at that.

'But I believe it's what's commonly called a love nest.'

Good Lord, not good. Definitely not good. She tried to act cool, unfazed, as if she wasn't embarrassed. As if the blood in her veins wasn't circling around her body and dispersing the kind of heat she associated with chilli peppers. 'I guess we should be thankful there aren't cherubs painted on the ceilings.'

'Wait till you see the bathroom.'

'No!' She swung to him. 'Cherubs?'

'Adam and Eve frolicking in the Garden of Eden, complete with strategically placed fig leaves.'

Oh, that was great, just great. She didn't want to share any apartment with Dominic, but to have to share this one?

She glanced across at him; her stomach tightened. According to rumour, women fell at his feet with tedious regularity. It was said that he picked them up, dusted them off, made love to them and then moved on with breathtaking speed. She had no intention of falling at any man's feet, least of all Dominic's, but... This apartment!

The claustrophobic cosiness made her want to flee. It should've been impossible to make such a large room claustrophobic, but it had been sectioned off to create cosy nooks.

She didn't want cosy nooks!

A pink velvet love seat reclined beneath one window, the same dusky colour as the drapes. A tiny pink sofa sat in front of the television unit, and she couldn't see how Dominic would fit into it on his own let alone with someone—that was, her—wedged in beside him.

A small dining table held pride of place in an intimate alcove. Four chairs stood around it, though she didn't see why the decorators hadn't dispensed with the pretence and ditched two of them. A ridiculously ornate chandelier hovered over it all.

The furniture was dainty, feminine and incredibly seductive. Her arms inched about her waist. The apartment crouched as if waiting to pounce and force her to unleash her rampant desires the moment she let her guard down.

Minky yowled and Bella jumped. She hastily removed the cat's cage from the coffee table and checked the satinwood for scratches. Dominic glanced at the cat and his lip curled as if he'd just stepped in something he wished he hadn't.

'Are you allergic?' she asked, half-hopefully. Maybe he'd choose a tent over sharing an apartment with a cat.

'No.'

Damn.

'But I don't like them.'

'Me, neither.' Minky glared at her. She glared right back. 'I'm more of a dog person.'

'Then why do we have a cat in our apartment?'

'It's not mine.' She transferred her glare to Dominic. She didn't like the way he'd emphasised the words *we* and *our* in that sentence, but didn't know how to say so without sounding like a stark, raving lunatic.

Who knew? Maybe she was a lunatic. Mel had lumped her with the cat, hadn't she?

'A favour for a friend.' She sighed. 'It should only be for a week, maybe two. If you really hate it that much, I'll put off moving to Newcastle until later.' Then she could get away from this God-awful apartment. It'd mean a long commute for the time being, but that was suddenly far more attractive than spending more time than necessary in this apartment. With Dominic.

'I can put up with the cat for a week or so.'

Fabulous.

She glanced around again and this time it was her lip that curled. 'This is my exact idea of what a brothel would look like.'

'I've never been in a brothel, so I can't help you out there.'

No, he would never have to pay for sex.

She stiffened and tried to banish that thought from her mind.

'I, uh… My father can't possibly be responsible for this apartment.'

'He wouldn't have organised it. His secretary's secretary would've booked the accommodation.'

Right. She thought about that for a moment. This so-called hiccup, this farce of an apartment, Dominic's reputation… She tried to keep her voice casual. 'You don't happen to know this particular secretary's secretary by any chance?'

He stilled. Then he swung around, his eyes narrowed. He folded his arms. Each movement made muscles ripple. 'Are you asking me if I've slept with your father's secretary's secretary?'

She gave up on being casual. 'I'm wondering if there's someone in the chain who would find this amusing.' Exactly how many hearts had he broken? How many women were there out there who wouldn't mind the chance for a little payback?

His lip curled. 'You've been listening to gossip.'

'Warnings,' she countered.

House rules. Ground rules. Now.

'You have a reputation, Dominic. A reputation any woman would be a fool to ignore. I've been told you break women's hearts as easily as you snap your fingers. That it's all a game to you.'

His mouth opened but no sound came out.

'I'm a woman, I have a heart and now I'm stuck in this God-awful apartment with you for who knows how long. Believe me, I mean to heed the warnings.'

He slammed his hands to his hips. 'And just like that my character is condemned?'

'I'm not condemning you.' She took a step back. 'But you're a confirmed bachelor, right?'

'There isn't anyone more confirmed.'

'Marriage is…?'

'A dirty word.'

'Whereas me, I'm a hearts-and-flowers kind of girl all the way—marriage, babies, the works. That's what I want.'

She tried to laugh but her eyes had dipped below shoulder level and the laugh caught in her throat. With his legs planted firmly apart they looked longer, firmer. The loose, low-slung cut of his jeans couldn't hide the power of his thighs. Bella's fingers flexed and curled.

She wanted to look away, but she couldn't. Her cheeks started to burn. She dragged her eyes up to his face. His hair was a halo of fiery reds and golds. Temptation personified. She shook herself. 'Are you telling me your reputation is unearned?'

'I'm telling you that it's irrelevant.'

Really? She might not be all that experienced where men were concerned, but in her father's office last week she'd noticed the way Dominic's eyes had kept travelling the length of her legs whenever he thought she wasn't watching. Then there'd been the speculation in their depths, their heat, when they'd rested on her mouth. It had sent an answering heat surging through her. She knew enough to know that meant trouble. She meant to cut it dead in its tracks.

'So…strictly business?'

'Strictly business,' he confirmed.

'Do you appreciate straight talking, Dominic?'

'I do.'

'Then I have to say that walking around half-naked doesn't seem to me the height of professionalism.'

'My walking around without a shirt bothers you?'

She refused to lie. 'It does.'

With a tightening of his lips, he turned on his heel and stalked from the room. He returned a moment later wearing a loose T-shirt that hung below his hips.

Had she offended him? She bit her lip. She couldn't afford to get him offside. She'd need his support if she were to bring her dream restaurant into being. She'd need his good opinion if she wanted to make her father proud. If he told Papa that she was a failure, that she was stupid… She gulped and refused to follow that line of thought. 'Thank you,' she murmured.

He didn't say anything. Then, 'I left you the master bedroom.'

She swallowed. 'That was kind.'

'You might want to reassess that opinion once you've seen it.'

That didn't sound promising.

'Is this all your luggage?' He motioned to the bags. 'Or do you have more downstairs?'

'These aren't mine, they're the cat's.' Her gear was still in the boot of her car.

'What?'

She kicked a bag. 'We have dry food, tinned food, special treat food. We even have cat chocolate.'

He stared at her as if he didn't know what to say. She didn't blame him.

'Then there's her basket, her blankets, her toys. This cat even has a different DVD for each day of the week. I'm supposed to set them to play on continuous mode whenever I go out so she doesn't get lonely. This is the blasted prima donna of all cats. Do you still think you can put up with it?'

'Yes.' But he ground the word out between his teeth.

'Tell me we have a DVD player in the apartment or I'll have to race home and grab mine.' Which could be a good thing. A chance for fresh air...

'There's a DVD player.'

He shifted his weight and shoved his hands in his pockets. He might've covered up, but Bella could recall with irritating clarity the definition of his pecs and abs, and how firm and warm his skin had felt against her cheek.

'What'll happen if it doesn't get its DVD?'

She shook herself and hauled her gaze back to the cat. 'She'll destroy the apartment, that's what.'

'Why'd you agree to look after the damn thing?'

Even twisted up like that his lips looked intriguing and full of promise. 'Because Melanie is my friend and nobody else would do it.'

'I don't like the sound of that.'

'Minky's cantankerous.'

His lip curled. 'Minky?'

'Don't even go there. Not my cat. I didn't name her.'

His lips twitched. 'What would you call her?'

'Medusa,' she growled. 'Because I'm petrified every single time she looks at me.'

He laughed then and all his beguiling goldenness and warmth seemed to reach out and brush against her. Her heart surged against her ribcage. Her lungs contracted.

'If you give me your car keys I'll go get your bags.'

Without a word, she fished her keys out of her pocket and handed them over. She wasn't sure she was capable of speech.

When he left, she had to draw in several gulps of air before she could force her mind to work again. Bedroom. *That's right, check out the bedroom.*

A short hallway led to two bedrooms directly opposite each other with the bathroom at the end. She peered in at the door on her right, and her jaw dropped. The rest of the apartment maintained a loose French Regency theme but this… This was just plain tacky.

She hated hot pink.

She checked out the bathroom. 'Pah!' She walked back to stare at the bedroom. Her worst nightmare, that was what this was. This bedroom, this apartment and the man she had to share it with.

'Oh, hell, Bella. How many bags did you bring?' Dominic struggled back into the apartment and dropped her bags to the living-room floor.

'We're in Newcastle for two months, remember?' She gestured to her bedroom. 'This is… It's… I…' She couldn't find words.

'Yeah, I know. And I'm not swapping.'

'Is that supposed to be a bed?' She motioned to the round concoction smack-bang in the middle of the room, heaped with hot-pink cushions and surrounded by pastel-pink mosquito netting.

'I guess.'

She swung to his room. Its blankness shocked her: stark walls. Stark furnishings. She glanced back at her room, then his. It didn't make sense. Overdone, overblown and tacky to cold, clinical and utilitarian? Not that Dominic had added any personal touches either. Her eyes narrowed. The room didn't even hint at the personality of the man who inhabited it.

Not that she really knew much about his personality, she had to admit, only what the gossips had told her. But she knew enough to know he was a sensualist, like her. They chose to express it in different ways, that was all. He through sex; she through food. Together they could...

Don't go there! Dominic conquered women the way the Roman Empire had conquered new territory—with a brash ruthlessness and half an eye on new horizons. Bella didn't want to be conquered. She sure as hell didn't want to be left for a new horizon.

'Bella?'

She shook herself and gestured to his bedroom. 'I don't like that any better.'

'You don't?'

'It's awful.'

He pointed to her room. 'Worse than that?'

'Just as bad. Why don't you put some things around?'

'Like?'

'I don't know. Like a colourful quilt or something. Some photos... Anything.'

'We're only here for two months.'

Only two months? It stretched out like an eternity for her.

'I like things neat.'

'That's not neat,' she blurted out. 'It's blank!'

She tried to read the expression in his eyes. He couldn't seriously like that room, could he? She understood his masculine pride baulking at the hot pink, but...

She glanced back at his room. He didn't live like that normally, did he? At that thought something shifted inside her, but she couldn't name what it was.

Only, she recognised that blankness. She and her father had felt that blank after her mother had died.

CHAPTER FOUR

'OKAY, time to discuss house rules.'

Bella pushed away from Dominic's intriguing proximity. He'd moved in beside her to shake his head once again at the hideousness of her bedroom, his arm almost touching hers. It made her jumpy.

She didn't want jumpy. She didn't want the blood stampeding through her veins as his cinnamon scent infiltrated her senses either. She wanted—needed—her mind honed and zeroed in on her goal.

A man who thought marriage a dirty word was not going to distract her from that.

'House rules?'

Bella had almost reached the end of the hallway. She turned to find that Dominic hadn't moved. He raised an eyebrow. She swallowed. She had to find a way to live and work with this man. The sooner she did that, the sooner she could focus on the important things, like putting her plans for her father's dream restaurant into action and making him proud of her. Making amends. 'House rules,' she repeated in as firm a tone as she could muster.

Which was pretty firm. She was kind of proud of it. She'd bet Dominic was used to women rushing to fulfil his every whim. Not her, though. No way. That would not be the way to earn his respect. It certainly wouldn't be a way to keep things on a business footing either.

'You may well be the boss when we're at work, Dominic, but here—' she slapped a wall '—we're equals. But coffee first, I think, yes?'

She headed for the living room. 'And then I best let Minky out of her cage.' She was hoping that, given more time, the cat would settle down and mellow out. She came to a halt and glanced around. Where on earth was the kitchen?

As if he could read her mind, Dominic came up behind her and pointed to a door discreetly set into the wall near the dining nook. She had to look twice before she could make it out.

Right. She set off for it.

The kitchen wasn't large, but it was well-appointed. A gleaming new red-and-chrome coffee machine sat on the bench in front of her. She stroked it with one finger and then reached up and pulled a packet of coffee beans from a cupboard above her head.

Dominic blinked. 'How'd you know that was there?'

'My father organised this apartment, right? Or at least, his secretary's secretary did. But he'd have given instructions.' Though Papa's lip would curl as much as hers and Dominic's if he ever saw the place. Still, she had no intention of ringing to complain. Low maintenance, that was what she had to be. Low maintenance, adult and businesslike. She should write that down and repeat it three times every day.

Besides, if this wasn't somebody's idea of a joke or a payback, then…

Katie, her father's secretary, was going through a terrible divorce. Bella recalled that late file and shook her head. Katie had enough on her plate at the moment. Bella wasn't going to complain. She had no intention of adding to Katie's troubles.

'So?'

She snapped to. 'This is the cupboard above the coffee machine. The coffee beans are always in the cupboard above the coffee machine.' She pointed to a cupboard behind him. 'That should be full of red wine. Nice red wine,' she added.

He opened the cupboard, pulled out a bottle and his eyebrows shot up. 'This is good stuff.'

'He'll have stocked it from his personal cellar. There'll be a box of expensive chocolates in the fridge, too, even though I keep telling him not to store them there, along with my favourite brand of cooking chocolate.'

He opened the fridge door. He closed it again. 'You're right on both counts.'

She shrugged and turned back to the coffee machine. 'He knows all my weaknesses.'

'And he likes to ensure you have everything you could possibly want.'

He spoke the words lightly, but she caught the thread of steel beneath them, the contempt. She knew exactly what he thought—that she was spoiled and wilful, that she took advantage of her father.

Bella is spoiled... Her heart stuttered in her chest. Her father's only rewards for all his generosity was disappointment and pain. She whirled around. 'Yes, my father is generous to a fault, but you can't tell me you haven't been a recipient of his generosity either.'

He blinked and sort of frowned, as if he couldn't work her out.

'Because I know you have. I did some research on you, Dominic Wright.'

Just for a moment she could've sworn he stiffened, and then he grinned the grin that transformed him from The Iceman into a golden devil. He moved to the bench beside her, rested back against it. 'And what did you come up with?'

He maintained a reasonable distance but the scent of cinnamon curled around her. She tore open the packet of coffee beans and their fragrance spilled into the kitchen, chasing the cinnamon away.

'I found out that he hired you a good year before you finished your university degree. He took a risk on you then.'

'A gamble that paid off.'

'And that until this week you've been working in acquisitions and mergers.' And from all accounts he'd been doing brilliantly there. She met his eyes with a challenge of her own. 'But it has to be said, acquisitions and mergers isn't exactly the kind of area that qualifies you as project manager for the Newcastle Maldini. My father is, again, obviously taking a gamble on you.'

He shifted, straightened. 'Are you saying you doubt my capacity to discharge my duties adequately?'

Adequately? Pah! She ground the coffee beans, the noise providing her with an excuse to remain silent.

'Bella?' His voice was hard.

'I'm saying that I'm not taking it for granted.'

She made the coffee. She took hers black and unsweetened. 'Milk? Sugar?' When he shook his head, she pushed one mug across to him. 'And I want more than you merely discharging your duties *adequately*. The hotel's success is important to me.'

'Why?'

'I already told you. It was a dream that was important to both my parents.'

His too-perceptive eyes narrowed. 'I think there's more to it than that.'

And just like that she felt as if she were in a job interview. Her nerves skittered and skated. If there was one thing she hated passionately it was job interviews. She had no intention of sharing her real reasons with Dominic, her personal reasons. Her make-her-father-proud reasons. She wanted distance. A lot of distance. They might be physically stuck in this apartment, but they didn't have to share the same headspace.

It didn't change the fact she had to give him something. He was her boss. 'Why do you want to oversee this particular project?' she countered. 'Why the change?'

'A new challenge.'

She recognised the evasion. She and Dominic might not

have a lot in common, but they both liked to keep their cards close to their chests. And it had to be said, he did have a very nice chest. She shook that thought away. 'Same here.'

His eyes mocked her. 'Right.'

She waited for him to challenge her further, but he just shrugged. 'Do you mean to leave that cat in its cage all day?'

She bit back a sigh and, mug in hand, made for the living room. Setting her mug on the coffee table, she knelt down beside the cage. 'Hey there, Minky,' she said in as conciliatory a voice as she could manage. 'You are going to be a good kitty-cat, aren't you?'

Soothing and calm, she instructed herself. She needed the cat to feel secure and unthreatened in its new environment. She hunkered down until she was almost eye level with the feline. 'We'll take it slow, okay? I'll open the door and you can wander on out whenever you feel like it to check out your new home. And then I'll get you some dinner, okay? How's that sound?'

'Like far more explanation than anything with four legs needs,' Dominic drawled.

'Ignore the nasty man,' Bella told the cat in the same sing-song, hopefully soothing voice.

Minky's yellow-green eyes glared at her. The tail swished. Good Lord, who was she trying to kid? The cat hated her.

She glanced up at Dominic. 'I'm not exactly sure how she'll react. She's, um, not happy.'

'It's a cat,' he dismissed. 'It weighs, what? Two kilos at the most? It can't exactly do that much damage.'

She pointed at him. 'Famous last words.' He grinned and it lifted something inside her. With heart thumping, she opened the cage door.

Minky exploded from it like a demented jack-in-the-box on steroids to claw straight up Dominic's denim-clad legs. He'd moved to stand in front of the cage, Bella presumed so he could get a better view of the show, but he didn't deserve that.

'Minky!' She leapt up.

Yowling, the cat let go and then proceeded to bounce off the sofa, the coffee table and two dining room chairs before settling under the television cabinet, eyes glaring and tail twitching in compulsive malevolence.

Bella armed herself with a cushion before spinning back to Dominic. 'Did she hurt you?' Her eyes dropped to his thighs. Five tiny pinpricks of blood stained the denim of his jeans—three on the left thigh and two on the right. Her mouth dropped open. 'Oh, I am sorry!'

It took all of Dominic's willpower not to harden under Bella's dark-eyed gaze. Damn schizoid cat! 'It's nothing,' he dismissed.

Bella glanced at him, at the cat, at the sofa and finally at the rug. Clutching the cushion to her chest, she carefully lowered herself to the floor, one eye firmly on the demon cat from hell. Not that he blamed her. Still, it was obvious she'd rather take her chances on the floor with the cat than on the sofa with him.

A scowl built through him. Her insinuation that he'd slept with whoever had organised this apartment, her obvious suspicion that he attempted to seduce every woman that crossed his path, still stung. The glance she sent him, however, made him feel like the wolf of Red Riding Hood fame. He lowered his frame to the sofa, stretched out his legs and fought a frown. Did she think he meant to jump her the moment she let her guard down? He had more finesse, more style, than that.

Besides, he had no intention of trying to seduce her—regardless of how tantalising the idea might seem. This lady was one complication he didn't need.

She surveyed him over the rim of her coffee cup. 'We should set some house rules.'

He shifted back, alternately straightening and slouching, but the sofa refused to give way to the shape of his body. 'We should?'

'Sure we should.'

He stuffed a cushion behind his back. 'Like?'

'Like, do you have any pet hates other than cats?'

He stopped his shuffling. 'You're not going to ask me to do anything for that blasted cat are you?' He pulled the cushion back out and tossed it to the floor.

'No.'

Her eyes darted to his thighs again. He bit back a groan and wished he'd kept hold of that sandbag of a cushion. He wanted to make Bella pay for all the heartache she'd caused Marco, but not in *that* way. Then he recalled the look on her face when she'd whirled around to him and pointed out that he'd been a recipient of Marco's generosity, too. The lift of her chin when she had claimed the hotel's success was important to her.

He didn't know what to make of it.

'What about you? Any pet hates?'

Her eyes lifted from his thighs and he found he could breathe again, after a fashion. 'I hate cheerful chat in the mornings. In fact, I'd really rather you didn't speak to me at all before I've had at least one cup of coffee, preferably two.'

'What constitutes cheerful?'

'Anything more than a grunt.'

All his tightness dissolved. A laugh built inside him.

'Seriously, Dominic, I'm not joking.'

The laugh burst free and something shifted inside him, deeper than his desire but not as intense.

A warning bell suddenly went off in his head. Bella had the same soft, melt-a-man-where-he-stood eyes that his father had always fallen for—eyes that turned grown men into pathetic, grovelling saps.

Nobody was turning him into a sap!

'Mornings aren't my strong suit.'

He'd bet she'd look deliciously rumpled in the mornings.

'So what do you hate in a flatmate?' she persisted.

He snapped to. 'I don't know. I've never had one.'

Her jaw dropped. She leant forward. 'What? Never? What about when you were at university?'

'I lived off campus.'

He'd lived in a caravan park with his father because by then someone had had to look after him, and everyone else had deserted him—including all those doe-eyed women who'd manipulated him time after time until Dominic hadn't been able to watch any more.

He'd sworn never to let a woman reduce him to that kind of dependence, that kind of pathetic wretchedness and despair. He'd looked after his father throughout his alcoholism and associated dementia. After that he'd decided roommates were a bad idea.

Bella frowned as if she'd read that thought in his face. 'But you must've been on other business trips like this?'

'Never for this long. If a team of us shot off somewhere, it was only ever for a few days. We'd stay in hotels and have our own rooms.'

She stared at him for a long moment and then shook herself. 'So how do you want to do things?'

'What things?'

'Food, for a start. We have to eat.'

'We can have groceries delivered.'

'Uh-huh. And who's going to cook them?'

He stared at her for a moment and then it hit him. She thought he was an unreconstructed, sexist Neanderthal who was going to lump her with all the housework!

Big bad wolf *and* sexist Neanderthal?

He forced down an angry denial and leaned back, the epitome of casual unconcern. 'Well, now, Bella, since you're the chef...'

Her chin shot up. 'You are not lumping me with all the cooking. I'll be doing enough of that throughout the day.'

'But the restaurant doesn't open for another two months.'

'So? I'll be training staff, checking out our suppliers, putting the chefs through their paces.'

He rubbed a hand across his jaw. 'Couldn't you get one of

the minions to whip us up something we could reheat when we got home?'

'I'll do that just as soon as you ask the hotel's housemaids to come around and take care of our ironing!'

Devilry sparked through him. 'Now there's an idea.'

Her jaw dropped. He laughed outright. Her eyes narrowed. He waited for her to realise her mistake—that he wasn't the unreconstructed male that she made him out to be. Instead she folded her arms and said, 'I will not be taken advantage of.'

He shook his head. Unbelievable. 'How about we take it in turns to cook, then?' She couldn't find fault with that plan, could she?

'Can you cook?'

She'd pay for that. 'Guess you'll find out.'

She scrutinised him with the intensity of a magnifying glass frying a bug in the sun. The big bad wolf and Red Riding Hood analogy sprang into his mind again and it took all his effort not to yell at her to stop looking at him like that.

'I bet you're used to women fussing around you, wanting to service your every need.'

She'd pay double for that crack.

She pointed a finger at him. 'This is a work environment!' Precisely.

'What I mean is… It's just…' She blew a strand of hair out of her face. 'Look, we share the household chores and the only other thing…'

She glanced away. He leaned forward, intrigued. 'The only other thing?'

Her chin lifted but she didn't meet his eye. 'I don't think you should bring your dates back here, that's all,' she finished in a rush.

Her opinion of him wasn't just bad, it was appalling! For a moment he couldn't even speak.

'If you were sharing this apartment with my father, would you bring women back?'

No, he damn well wouldn't. Just as he had no intention of doing so now. He couldn't credit her with deliberately trying to offend him, but he had every intention of making her pay for her unjust assessment of him. *Every* intention. Someone should teach Bella the dangers of jumping to conclusions.

'I think you'll find, Bella—' he all but purred her name and had the satisfaction of seeing her swallow '—that I will be the model flatmate. To prove my point, why don't I take care of dinner tonight?'

She moistened her lips, staring up at him with big eyes, like those of a deer caught in the headlights. 'That's not necessary.'

'Oh, I think it is.'

She clutched her cushion closer. 'Okay, then. Lovely.'

The look on her face told him she suspected it wasn't nourishment but seduction that he had planned. He sent her a cat-that-got-the-cream grin that was designed to keep her thinking exactly that. 'Dinner will be served at seven-thirty.'

'Lovely,' she repeated.

But the expression on her face said the opposite and it was all he could do not to laugh.

'Let the games begin.'

Dominic lit the single-tapered candle, stepped back to survey the arrangement and grinned. A white damask cloth draped the table and fell in soft folds to the floor. Crystal and silver gleamed in the candlelight sending an intimate glow throughout the apartment.

He'd spent an age consulting with Jean-Claude about the meal tonight. He'd wanted a menu that would knock Bella's socks off.

And he had it.

He couldn't wait to see her face when she saw it, tasted it.

At the idea of her mouth closing around the food he'd chosen, savouring it, his gut clenched. Images bombarded him. He pushed them away. He had every intention of seducing Bella's senses through the food and wine, through the atmosphere he'd created, but it was a mock seduction only. Although she thought otherwise, Bella was as safe as houses.

He meant to enjoy watching her squirm.

Then succumb to his charm.

And then realise her mistake.

A glance at his watch told him it was time. He tapped on her door and had to bite back a grin when it flew open immediately, as if she'd been waiting on the other side. Then the grin slid right off his face. What the...?

She raked him up and down with her hot, brown gaze and then scowled right back at him. 'Don't look at me like that,' she snapped. 'You didn't tell me this was formal, so it's not my fault.'

He didn't care that she'd elected to dress casually. It was the kind of casual she'd chosen that irked him. Perspiration prickled his scalp. She seemed to scream, *big bad wolf.*

'What is that?' He motioned to what she wore. He shouldn't have asked, but he couldn't help it.

'A track suit,' she returned with the kind of slow deliberation reserved for the bovine. Then she stifled a yawn. 'Is dinner ready?'

He nodded.

A track suit? It was the baggiest track suit known to man. It was so baggy she could share it with three other people and still have room to house a small African nation.

The dismal colour did nothing for the clear brilliance of her skin either. Grey. It wasn't even a deliberate grey, but one of those greys that looked as though it had been through the washing machine too many times. The women he knew wouldn't be seen dead in an outfit like that.

Without a scrap of make-up and her hair pulled into a high ponytail, she looked all of sixteen.

Big bad wolf!

Irritation inched up his backbone. He wasn't some slathering beast waiting to fasten his jaws about her delectable throat.

'Are you going to let me out?'

He shook himself and stepped back and swept a gallant arm down the short hall. At least, he hoped it was gallant. All his muscles had bunched and stiffened as if they didn't belong to him any more.

Manners; charm, he ordered. She'd be putty in his hands soon enough. He slipped past her to hold out her chair but she'd halted to seize the remote from the coffee table and click on the television.

'Do you mind?' She glanced up. 'There's a documentary that sounds—'

'Yes, I do mind.' He snatched the remote and clicked the television off again. 'I've gone to all this trouble. The least you can do is appreciate it and pretend to enjoy it.'

'Trouble?' She raised an eyebrow. 'What? You set the table?'

Nope, the waiter had taken care of that when he'd delivered the food. Dominic dropped his hands to her shoulders and propelled her to her seat. His outrage dissolved as her warmth crept through the thin cotton of her top and seeped into his hands. How many times had this thing been through the washing machine? It was so thin he could...

He snatched his hands back. He needed to remain cold and clinical if he was going to pull this off.

'I know you haven't actually cooked anything. Cooking a lovely meal, now that takes commitment.' She drew the word out like a taunt. 'I promise, when you make that sort of effort, I'll appreciate it.'

At her words the feast in the kitchen suddenly developed a kind of moral mould, became cheap and self-indulgent. He gave himself a mental kick. Hell, no! It wasn't cheap. It was the best money could buy.

'You know, if you were doing take-out I'd have been just as happy with pizza.'

Pizza? *Pizza!* He tried to hide his indignation. 'I'll have you know this isn't just any take-out.'

'Oh?'

He pulled in a breath and tried a different tack, but then her scent slammed into him, all lemon zest and tang. 'I wanted to make things nice for you.' His jaw clenched. 'Special,' he ground out.

Charm, remember? Had he seriously thought seducing her—pseudo-seduction or otherwise—would be easy?

A soft touch she wasn't, but the challenge fired his blood. 'I wanted to celebrate.'

She stifled another yawn. 'Celebrate what?'

'The beginning of our working relationship,' he said smoothly, keeping his voice low and intimate. He lifted the bottle chilling on ice. 'Champagne?'

'Is it French?' she demanded, with a supercilious lift of one eyebrow. 'I only drink French.'

He gritted his teeth and then pulled in a breath. 'Naturally.' He'd manage suave and charming if it killed him. She could shrug and yawn all she liked. What she'd get in return was cultured and courteous. Determination settled over him. He'd impress her with this meal. He'd impress her with his manners. He'd break down the barriers she'd erected, and he'd make her laugh, joke and spar with him and enjoy herself. He'd make her see he *wasn't* a beast.

'How do you know I haven't cooked?' He was honestly curious.

She sipped the champagne before answering. It left a shine on her lips and he found it difficult to drag his gaze away. She might've scorned make-up and glamorous clothing, but her bearing, her gestures, betrayed her innate sensuality. She moved with the fluid grace and assurance of a confident woman.

'There are only finished-meal smells, no cooking smells.'

He blinked.

'Plus, cooking is noisy and the apartment has been quiet all evening.'

Aha. So she had been aware.

'You ought to serve the fish before it dries out.'

How the hell?

'I can smell it,' she said before he could ask.

She was a chef. Of course she could smell it.

She flipped out her napkin and smoothed it across her lap then raised an eyebrow. He jerked into action. He was supposed to be acting smooth, suave; serving food with finesse and style. Not standing there gaping at her like some uncouth teenager. Like a…

Like a sap!

He shot into the kitchen, braced his hands against a bench and counted to three.

He was not uncouth. He was not a sap. He was not a big bad wolf.

He *would* make her smile.

He opened his eyes, pushed his shoulders back and grabbed their plates. With a flourish he set the cod in white wine sauce in front of her, then slid into the seat opposite. Anticipation fired through him.

She sniffed. He leaned in closer, watching for the dreamy expression he'd imagined rippling across her face. If he had her pegged right, Bella would react to fine food the way other women reacted to jewellery.

'They've used oregano in the sauce instead of marjoram.' Her lips turned down. 'Why overpower the delicate taste of the fish like that?' Her clear eyes met his, disappointment etched in their depths. He lost the power to speak.

She picked up her fork, flaked off a small piece and brought it to her lips. He held his breath and waited. No dreamy expression appeared. Disappointment burned through him, hot and acrid.

As if she could feel his gaze, she glanced up and met it.

'It's nice and moist, though,' she said with a faintly resigned, 'it's what I expected' half smile, half grimace. As if she had to search her mind for a compliment to toss off as a sop to his ego.

As if he were a sap.

Dominic lost his appetite then and there.

CHAPTER FIVE

Oʜ ᴍʏ God! The fish was out-of-this-world delicious. It took all of Bella's willpower not to moan in pleasure as she forked another glorious morsel into her mouth. She nearly weakened altogether at Dominic's evident disappointment, but hastily pulled herself up. Weaken now, and she was lost. Conquered territory et cetera.

She didn't know how it was possible to stop becoming emotionally involved when one made love. She didn't know how Dominic managed it, and she didn't want to know his secret either. But when she made love, she wanted to give herself wholeheartedly.

Oh, she knew some movies, books and pop songs exaggerated the link between love and sex, but it was only possible to exaggerate something that already existed. And she felt the germ of truth in those movies, books and songs right down in her bone marrow. Right down in her heart.

She wanted to love the man she made love with. She wanted to be sure of his love for her.

She wanted 'for ever'.

Dominic and for ever? Ha! If she were lucky he might promise her to the end of next week.

Not good enough.

Even though Bella knew she was making the sensible decision, the right choice for her, her body kicked up a ruckus in protest. Her eyes burned. Her head started to ache.

And the rotten fish was delicious!

She'd resisted being lumped with all the cooking because, in her mind, cooking night after night for a man could become as dangerous as sleeping with him. If a woman wasn't careful, she could find herself building fantasies around him. Stupid fantasies.

If you ate night after night with a man, could you create stupid fantasies, too?

With an abrupt movement she set her plate on the floor for Minky. The delicious smells had brought her out of hiding and made her semi-amiable, at least for the moment.

'What the—?'

'Minky may be a prima donna,' she said with an airy wave of her hand, pretending not to notice his outrage, desperately trying to keep her hormones in check. 'But she won't notice the oregano, and if she does she won't care. What's for mains?'

She waited for him to slam his cutlery to his plate, explode at her for her rudeness and then storm out of the apartment. She wouldn't blame him, either. She didn't want to hurt his feelings, but the only way she'd ever managed subtle was in a sauce.

He was a womaniser, and he was ruthless. This was supposed to be a business arrangement, yet here he was taking full advantage of the situation. She sat back, hardened her heart. She would not be taken advantage of. She would not be distracted from what she wanted to achieve.

And, while she may be at a loss at how to keep him onside while keeping him at arm's length, from the moment she'd opened her bedroom door and found him standing there dressed to kill—in the rotten candlelight, no less—a part of her had decided he deserved everything she could throw at him tonight. And more.

All this glorious food was just part and parcel of an elaborate seduction. He wasn't interested in her as a woman, a person. He was interested in the challenge…and the body.

A pulse in her throat fluttered to life.

'The next course is a surprise,' he informed her with an ur-
banity that masked everything but the appreciative light in his
eyes as they rested on her face.

Man, he was good. She wanted to applaud his polish, his
cool. Instead, when he disappeared back into the kitchen with
their plates she seized the moment to rest her elbows on the
table, press her palms to her eyes and breathe deeply.

He returned with their main course. The smell hit her first,
then he set it down in front of her and her mouth watered with
the kind of ferocity she normally reserved for a good curry.

A lamb loin.

Stuffed.

With a crust.

She wanted to close her eyes and inhale its scent. Then
she wanted to savour every succulent morsel. She didn't. She
lifted her knife and fork, sent him a tight little smile, then cut
into the moist meat.

Oh, good Lord. Hot-knife-through-butter tender.

She brought a piece to her lips, aware of how closely he
watched her, as if by sheer willpower he could regulate her
responses.

She knew what response he wanted: her surrender.

Not in this lifetime, buddy.

She closed her mouth around the morsel of food…

Mamma Mia! She chewed and tried not to let the taste
transport her. By some miracle she managed to keep her face
wooden as she did her best to concentrate on the combination
of flavours, like a wine taster. Only, there was no way she was
spitting this out. It was way too good for that.

'How's the sauce?'

She almost laughed at the edge behind the polite enquiry.
'Actually, it's quite good.' Divine, really. 'I just don't understand why the chef chose cashews for the crust rather than pine
nuts.' Oh, yes, she did.

She feigned indifference as she took another bite. Minky

meowed. She pushed the cat away with the edge of her foot. No way; she wasn't sharing this. 'Pine nuts would've enhanced the texture and lifted this dish out of the ordinary.' *Not!*

'Ordinary?'

'Uh-huh.' She dabbed at her mouth with her napkin. Still he didn't explode. Instead he reached out and poured her a glass of red wine. She glanced at the label and dabbed at her mouth again. 'What made you choose a Merlot over a Cabernet Sauvignon?'

He slammed the bottle down, his eyes shooting sparks. 'I didn't choose it,' he ground out. 'The restaurant promised to provide an ideal wine with each course.'

She slammed her knife and fork to her plate and met his glare with one of her own. 'The restaurant? You didn't even choose the *wine* yourself?' Indignation shot through her. Had he done anything other than make a phone call? 'What does the restaurant know? Who is this restaurant anyway, if they're supposed to be so darn good?'

'The Regency Bellevue,' he ground out between clenched teeth. 'And they're the best.'

'Pah! My restaurant will be better than this.' She pushed her plate away in disgust. Not in disgust at the food—despite her boast, it'd take a lot of hard work to reach the same standard as the Regency Bellevue, hard work she was fully prepared to put in—but in disgust at Dominic. Did he really think he could seduce a woman without putting in a real effort?

'Is there no pleasing you?' Dominic snapped.

'I'd be well pleased if this was all innocent, a meal shared with a business colleague, but it's not innocent, is it?'

Her accusation brought him up short. While he had no intention of seducing her, he had done everything in his power to let her think he meant to. So, innocent? Not precisely.

He hadn't expected her to challenge him head-on, though. The women he knew played games, hedged and shifted, and would never issue such a direct challenge. Evidently Bella wasn't of their ilk.

'But if you're so hell-bent on seduction, at least put in a decent effort!'

He gaped. 'Decent effort?'

'What, beyond forking out an obscene amount of money that you can well afford, have you actually invested of yourself this evening?'

'Time and thought,' he shot back.

'Time, huh? How long did it take you to consult with the chef and decide on a menu? Fifteen minutes?'

He held her gaze but shifted on his seat again and her lips twisted.

'Ten minutes? And how much thought did you put into those ten minutes?'

He didn't say anything.

'And then the food was delivered by someone else, the table set by someone else. You just donned your glad rags and served it up and you expect me to applaud and think you're wonderful? I don't think so.' She sat back and folded her arms.

'A simple "thank you" would've sufficed.'

This time it was she who shifted on her chair, but she stared at him with eyes that screamed 'big bad wolf'. He'd been an idiot to play this game.

'I wasn't trying to seduce you,' he ground out.

Her eyes called him a liar.

How had this backfired so spectacularly? 'The conclusions you jumped to about me earlier... They annoyed me. You condemned me as a womaniser.'

Her eyes became less certain. 'Are you telling me you're not a womaniser?'

If he did it'd be an outright lie. He frowned. So why had he taken offence at the truth?

Because it wasn't true where she was concerned!

How was she supposed to know that?

He scowled and continued as if she hadn't spoken. 'And you wrote me off as some kind of unreconstructed jerk who was going to land you with all the household chores.'

She bit her lip.

'And you'd jumped to all those conclusions not based on any evidence of your own but because of hearsay and gossip.'

She stilled.

'So I decided to teach you a lesson. I thought I'd let you think seduction was precisely what I had on my mind.' He leaned across the table towards her. He eyes widened and her lemon tang taunted him. 'And at the end of the evening, when you were anticipating my main move...'

Her throat worked. 'Yes?'

'I was simply going to say good night and retire to my room alone. And leave you stewing in the realisation that you'd read me all wrong, that you'd judged me unfairly.'

She stared at him and something in her eyes flashed. 'Don't you think that's a stupidly elaborate charade to go through just to teach me a lesson? Why on earth didn't you tell me to just wake up to myself? Much simpler and more straightforward, don't you think? Why didn't you talk to me about it like an... an adult?'

'Because you weren't acting like an adult!' he exploded back at her. 'Because you kept acting like I was about to jump on you any moment like some bloody big bad wolf. All of that... *virginal* shrinking really got my back up and—'

He broke off when Bella flinched at his words. Even in the candlelight he could see colour flood her face. She refused to meet his eyes.

He stared, and kept right on staring. 'My God,' he finally breathed. 'You have to be joking me?'

The colour deepened. 'I have no idea what you're talking about,' she croaked, her voice dry and brittle. She still wouldn't meet his eyes.

No! It couldn't be... He stabbed a finger down on the table

between them. 'You can't seriously expect me to believe that you are a virgin?'

She glared at him then. 'I'm not asking you to believe anything!'

Bella Maldini was a virgin? Dominic shot back in his seat, folded his arms and glared. Hell! This woman should come with a warning sign, with flashing lights and alarm bells over her beautiful head.

A virgin!

Dominic steered well clear of virgins. He dragged both hands back through his hair and praised the powers that be that his intentions tonight hadn't veered towards a real seduction. If he'd seduced Bella for real...

He clenched his jaw. Virgins built sex up to be an amazing romantic oneness, a mingling of the souls. They confused sex with love. They hadn't learned yet that love was a myth. They hadn't learned yet to disassociate sex from love. Some women never did; Dominic steered well clear of them, too. He might be a womaniser, but he wasn't stupid.

A virgin? Perspiration broke out on his upper lip. He had a reputation as a heartbreaker, but he only slept with women who shared his views about sex. Anything else became too complicated.

He wasn't into complications.

He didn't want to be the man to shatter a woman's illusions.

He wasn't into tears and he wasn't into heartbreak. There was enough pain in the world as it was and he had no intention of adding to it. Light-hearted laughter and fun, an uncomplicated good time—that was his speciality. Ring him for that, and he'd be there in a flash. But for anything more? Forget it.

'A virgin,' he murmured again. Unbelievable.

Bella tossed her head and glared. 'So what if I am? What's wrong with that?'

'Nothing.' Absolutely nothing. But thank heavens he'd never

had any real intention of pursuing uncomplicated, light-hearted fun with Bella, that was all he could say.

Damn it! He didn't have a one-track mind. He and Bella needed to get this sex question settled. They were in Newcastle because they had a job to do. End of story.

'I owe you an apology.'

That snapped him to.

'I did come here thinking the worst about you,' she admitted. 'That wasn't fair and I'm sorry.'

Her apology took him off-guard. The spoiled little rich girl knew how to apologise? He'd accused her of misjudging him, but in that instant he wondered just how much he'd misjudged her, too. She obviously hadn't spent the last several years being a party girl like he'd thought.

'Apology accepted.' He couldn't mistake the relief that flitted across her face, and for some reason that made him feel more like a big bad wolf than anything else had so far today.

He clenched his hands. They were putting this sex question to bed once and for all. 'You were right to be on your guard, Bella. I do have a reputation and, while the gossips have no doubt exaggerated it, I shouldn't have blamed you for thinking what you did.'

'No,' she countered. 'I should've known better. I should've made up my own mind about you instead of listening to what other people said. You see, I hate it when people judge me based on who my father is. So I really, *really* should've known better than to do the same to you.'

For a moment he was at a loss and that so rarely happened that three additional beats went by before he found his voice again, which might have been why he blurted it out so badly. 'I have a no-sex policy with work colleagues.' It wasn't a hundred per cent true; he could recall a couple of temps he'd considered fair game. But in Bella's case it was 'lock it in the safe and throw away the key' true.

She leaned towards him. 'Really?'

He wished he didn't notice the way her breasts rose and fell beneath that awful track suit. 'Cross my heart.'

'So this—' she gestured around the apartment '—really is all business?'

'Absolutely.'

'Oh, that is good news!'

She beamed at him and it took all his power to keep his blood cool and his mind on her words rather than the shape of her mouth.

'Because, Dominic, there is so much I want to learn from you.'

He didn't close his eyes. He didn't groan. He told himself that eventually he wouldn't read a double meaning into everything she said.

Her grin widened. He didn't groan about that either, but one thing became startlingly clear—he didn't want to become all buddy-buddy with her. Business, plain and simple. No complications.

'So what did you get for dessert?'

He stared at her for a long moment. 'I respect your father in ways I doubt you could even begin to understand.'

Her smile faded. 'I'm not sure what it is you're trying to say.'

'You really think you're up for this?' He put as much incredulity into his voice as he could. 'You really think you can pull this restaurant job off?'

'Yes, I do.'

'Given your past form, you really think you're going to last the distance?'

Her chin lifted. 'Oh, I'm not the one who'll have any trouble on that score.'

He made his lip curl. 'Let me make my position plain. I have doubts about your ability to knuckle down and stick to anything, Bella. Serious doubts. It'd be better for all concerned, and it'd save us a whole load of trouble, if you just left now rather than a month down the track. I'd prefer it, in fact, if you'd leave right now.'

There was a long pause and then she raised one supercilious eyebrow. 'Well, well, who knew that one little virgin could have The Iceman in such a sweat?'

He wasn't sweating!

'I'm not going anywhere, Dominic.'

'Is that a promise?'

'It is.'

Then he meant to make sure she kept it.

Still, she looked just as irresistible when she was haughty and disdainful as when she was smiling and animated. He wanted to throw his hands in the air and stalk off. 'Lemon tart,' he said instead. 'I ordered lemon tart for dessert.'

She rose. 'I do hope you enjoy it.'

She was the one who stalked off.

He was the one left feeling like a heel.

CHAPTER SIX

AFTER three days Dominic's curiosity finally conquered him. He found his feet taking him in the direction of Bella's domain—the kitchen.

For the last three days he and Bella had both been so busy they'd barely spent any time in each other's company. For all their discussion about chores, they hadn't even eaten together. When they were both in the apartment, they hunkered over their individual folders and reports at opposite ends of the living room, him at the dining table, Bella on the love seat with a couple of small occasional tables. He had to hand it to her—so far she was working hard.

Maybe she would see this project through.

He tried to halt the doubts that immediately crowded his mind. After their first disastrous night, he'd been doing his best to keep an open mind. As far as he was concerned, though, actions spoke louder than words and Bella's past actions—her flitting from job to job, from place to place—didn't fill him with much confidence.

Still, in all fairness…

So far so good.

Pulling in a deep breath—he always needed a lot of oxygen whenever dealing with Bella—he eased the kitchen door open and glanced inside.

Then blinked.

He'd expected a lot of noise—the banging and clattering

of pots and pans, for a start. Plus, the life, the vigour that he'd glimpsed in Bella, had told him she'd laugh a lot—down here in her territory, that was, if not with him in their apartment. He'd thought that would lead to a relaxed atmosphere, lots of chat and laughter.

That wasn't the case at the moment.

The air was so thick with unspoken tension the walls seemed to vibrate with it. His eyes narrowed as he tried to read the situation. Bella stood on the far side of the room, her back rigid and her movements jerky as she unpacked a large crate of vegetables. Off to one side, Luigi, the head chef, sat at a desk with his shoulders hunched. Half-a-dozen chefs and kitchen hands worked quietly, casting her anxious looks from time to time.

His gaze returned to Bella. She carefully removed the vegetables from the crate one by one, studied them and then set them on the counter-top. Her shoulders were so tense he thought they might lock up. When the vegetables were unpacked, she rested her elbow on the crate and her head on her hand.

He took a step into the room. Was she ill? Before he could ask, she snapped upright, grabbed another crate from the floor and slammed it up onto the bench.

Whoa! He blinked. Luigi flinched, so did the chefs and kitchen hands. None of them had so far noticed him.

He pursed his lips, his eyes not leaving her agitated form. She didn't pull these vegetables from their box. She merely flicked through them, her movements becoming more and more harried. Something about the action reminded him of Marco before he was about to explode.

He back-tracked a step and then rapped on the door. Every head swung to him. 'Sorry to interrupt but, Bella, I need you round in Reception for a moment.'

She swung round and stared at him as if she hadn't quite understood his request.

'I need your signature on a delivery.'

She shook herself, wiped her hands on her chef's smock

and nodded. 'Yes, of course.' She made for him and the door with speed, as if she couldn't wait to get out of the kitchen.

She swept past him. He let the door swing shut then lengthened his stride to catch up.

Once out of the kitchen, she seemed to grow. Her back became ramrod straight. Her eyes grew stormy. Dominic's breath caught. He had a sudden image of how amazing it'd be to kiss her when she was in this mood, of what it would be like to capture her lips with his, to tease and cajole until her temper metamorphosed into passion. It'd be out of this world. It'd…

He nearly tripped up when he realised the direction of his thoughts. Virgin; Marco's daughter; business—*don't forget it!* He dragged in a breath but it only pulled Bella's lemon scent into his lungs, rousing his senses to full and hungry consciousness.

'What delivery?' she snapped when they reached Reception, turning on the spot and then whirling to face him. 'I don't see a delivery.'

He hooked his arm through hers and towed her into the office behind the reception desk, kicking the door shut with his heel. She'd said she wanted to learn from him. Fine. Lesson number one: staff communication. 'You want to tell me what's going on in the kitchen?'

It took only that to unlock her pent-up emotion. She flung her gloriously expressive arms in the air and a stream of what sounded suspiciously like Italian invective followed. 'Do you know what that imbecile has done? He's buying inferior, substandard market produce just because the market gardener is his brother-in-law!'

She paced up and down and lapsed into Italian once more. He caught the odd phrase. He let her vent—in just the same way as he let Marco vent, he realised. Things mattered a lot to Marco, and he took some things that he shouldn't personally. Bella might have more in common with her father than Dominic had given her credit for.

'No restaurant of mine is sub-standard anything!'

She glared at Dominic as if he'd dared to suggest otherwise. No way. Not him. Not when she looked liked that.

She stabbed a finger in the air. 'And no backhanded, palm-greasing, slime-ball of a head chef is going to ruin my restaurant!'

Those words, however, held no conviction. She dropped down into a chair. Something in his chest started to burn at the way her shoulders slumped. 'Bella—'

'Oh, God, don't say it!' She raised stricken eyes. 'Believe me, I can see the hypocrisy for myself.'

What the...?

'Luigi is a fabulous chef and a nice man. He's buying supplies from his brother-in-law to help his family out. How can I—*me*—criticise that? *Me* who has been given this job because I'm the boss's daughter!'

Ah...

Dominic shifted a chair so he sat opposite. 'Okay, for starters, let's take our own insecurities out of this and move on.'

She stiffened. 'I—'

He held up a hand. She closed her mouth. 'We all have the jobs we have for whatever reasons, so let's just take that as a given, okay?'

She pursed her lips and then gave a curt nod.

'Tell me, is it right that Luigi should help out his family?'

'The helping in itself isn't wrong,' she said slowly.

'I agree. But to help them out at the expense of the hotel?'

She shook her head. 'That's not right.'

'So what can be done about it?'

She pulled in a breath. 'It has to stop.'

'Bella?' She met his gaze. 'Someone needs to talk to the supplier. Who do you think that should be—you or Luigi?'

She thought about it. 'Me,' she finally said. 'Luigi's family might try to steamroll him. Also, it could be awkward for him, but as I'm the boss I have the final say and they can't blame Luigi for that.'

He sat back then and smiled.

She stared at him. 'It's that simple?'

He nodded. Her gaze slid away then and a blush lit her cheeks. 'I'm sorry for all that.' She waved a hand to where she'd paced and vented. 'I panicked.'

'It's never a good idea to bottle up your concerns and then storm around the place like a passive-aggressive time bomb that's waiting to go off. Believe me, you don't want to alienate your staff.'

He watched his words sink in, watched neat white teeth emerge to chew her bottom lip.

'In a hotel like the Maldini, staff morale and teamwork are of the utmost importance. Bella, I can't stress that enough. Teamwork and team spirit will be crucial to our success.'

Bella glanced across at Dominic and suddenly understood why her father held him in such high esteem. She leaned towards him. 'Okay, how's this for a plan? I'll ask Luigi to set up a meeting between me and his brother-in-law.'

She chewed her bottom lip as she considered her options. She lifted her gaze to find Dominic studying the action and her lips with an intensity that almost blew the top off her head. He stared at them as if... As if...

As if he wanted to drag her to the floor and make wild passionate love to her! Heat pulsed to life in her abdomen. She shot back in her chair, her heart pounding. Dominic snapped back too, the pulse at the base of his jaw working furiously.

The sudden distance made no difference. Her thoughts scattered to the four winds. The air between them sizzled with the unspoken and the forbidden. And, for the first time in her life, Bella hungered for the forbidden. Completely and utterly. Without reservation. The realisation turned everything she knew about herself on its head.

She stared up into Dominic's blue-eyed goldenness and wondered what it would be like to be kissed by him. A crazy thought because, despite all her resolutions, she had a feeling that she wouldn't be able to stop at just one kiss. She may not be able to stop at just kisses.

'Bella?' Her name growled from his throat.

'Hmm?'

'This meeting with the supplier?'

Each word snapped out of him and his barely leashed anger pulled her from her trance. Oh, dear Lord. She pressed cool hands to overheated cheeks and did her best to gather her wits, her train of thought. *Luigi; produce; kitchens.*

'Um, right. I was thinking, what if I explain to Luigi's brother-in-law why the produce isn't up to scratch and then outline what standard I do need? If he can't supply it I'll tell him I'll be using someone else until he can. Once he can provide what I need, he can have my trade again. It might give him something to strive towards.'

He gave a curt nod. 'It sounds like a good plan.'

He still looked angry. She didn't want him angry. She wanted him...

No, no she didn't *want* him. She couldn't *want* him. But she'd like to rid him of that tight hardness. She'd like to dispel the tension.

'Or, of course, I could send him round to the Regency Bellevue as they're obviously not so fussy.'

He stared at her for a moment and then he grinned. It made her heart stutter. It made her want to grin back like an idiot. She didn't. At least, she hoped she didn't.

'It sounds as if you have it all under control.'

He stood.

She did, too. They both took a step away from each other. She knew the smart thing would be to leave. Pronto. But first...

'Dominic, thank you for taking the time to talk me through all that. I appreciate it.'

'It's what I'm here for.'

He worked harder than any person she'd ever met. He had high expectations of those in his employment, but they were no higher than the expectations he held for himself. Yet he'd developed a rapport with his staff—a combination of mutual respect, humour and open communication. He might hold himself aloof from romantic relationships, but he was far from unapproachable.

He made it look so easy.

It gave her hope.

'My people skills might need improving,' she confessed.

'A little,' he agreed. 'But you're getting on-the-job training and plenty of practice. You'll improve and it'll get easier with time.'

She had to get out of here now. It was simply too hard talking to him without touching him. 'Well, thanks for the pointers. I'll give them a go and see how I get on.'

'You do that.'

His eyes had gone dark again and it made her mouth dry. She tried to swallow but nearly choked when his gaze lowered to her lips. Again. A quiver trembled through her. 'Are we, uh, done here?'

'For the moment.'

She turned and made for the door, praying her legs would make it that far. It wasn't a given. Not when Dominic stared at her like that, like a man starving, aching…craving for a taste of her. *Her!*

Luckily her legs had the strength to take her all the way back to the kitchen. When she reached the kitchen doors, she pressed her back into the wall beside them and took three deep breaths. What would have happened if, instead of walking away, she'd walked across to him and lifted her face towards his and invited his kiss?

Parts of her grew so hot she thought she might melt down. Damn it! What had happened in Dominic's past? Something had to have happened. Something bad too, to make him avoid relationships the way he did. She thought of that blank canvas of a bedroom of his and an ache started up somewhere in the region of her chest.

In the next instant, she waved a hand in front of her face. What on earth was she thinking? She didn't want a relationship with Dominic Wright.

You want him to kiss you.

Hormones, that was all that was. And she had no intention of becoming a slave to them. Since she'd hit puberty—a cynical person would say since she'd developed breasts—she'd had first boys then men throwing her lures, attempting to seduce her. So far, she'd resisted. It was only now she realised why it'd been so darn easy.

No one had seriously tempted her before.

At least, no more than chocolate or a nice red wine.

Dominic was different. Dominic was a full gourmet meal, with an expensive bottle of champagne thrown in. He was moonlight, starlight and a full symphony orchestra.

Her hands clenched. How unfair was it that her first taste of real temptation should come in the shape of Dominic Wright? After all, there was temptation, then there was *Temptation*. And Dominic was the 'capital T' kind.

And the love 'em and leave 'em kind, she reminded herself. She had to keep her mind on her plans, her future and nothing else.

Still, there was no denying that—

No 'still'! No anything!

She rested her head back against the wall for a moment and then pushed herself upright and into the kitchen. She clapped her hands to get everyone's attention. 'Okay, you've all worked hard this morning, why don't you take a break?' She turned to her head chef. 'Before you race off, Luigi, may I have a word?'

She saw him swallow. 'Of course, *Signora* Bella.'

'Signorina,' she corrected with a smile and then waited

until the kitchen had emptied. She waved an arm at the boxes of vegetables that his brother-in-law had delivered this morning. 'Do you think I could meet with your brother-in-law?'

He eyed her uncertainly.

'I'm disappointed in the quality of the produce he sent. Now, Luigi, I'm not blaming you for it. I don't want you to think that. But I would like to meet with your brother-in-law so I can show him the standard of produce I require for this restaurant and see if he can provide it. If he can't, then we will need to start using another supplier until he can.'

He blinked and then he suddenly beamed at her. 'I will call him right now, *Signorina* Bella. *Pronto.*'

On Friday evening, Dominic stalked into the apartment carrying his briefcase, laptop and a brightly wrapped present. The present was rectangular in shape and, while not large, looked heavy. And festive, in its lime-green wrapping and yellow ribbon.

Bella couldn't help herself. 'Is it someone's birthday?' Was he about to head out again?

'It's for you.'

'For me?'

He handed it over and she discovered she'd been right—it was heavy for its size. 'For me?' she said again. Why would Dominic give her a gift?

'When I mentioned that it was a gift, the sales girl insisted on wrapping it.'

Bella just bet she had. Women were always going that extra mile for Dominic. She shook it. Nothing rattled. 'What is it?'

His lips twitched. 'Open it and see.'

Intrigued, she tore off the ribbon and paper. What on earth could he have bought her? The ribbon fell to the floor; the paper fell to the floor.

Bella stared.

Books. He'd bought her two books.

One was a dark blue hardcover about the theory and practice of leadership. She flicked through and her stomach clenched at the chapter headings: *Contemporary Strategy Analysis*; *Performance Appraisals; Managerial Economics*. She gulped. She'd never make heads nor tail of it.

'I found it one of the most useful textbooks when I was at university. I thought you might find it helpful, too.'

Helpful? She smiled and hoped it hid her sudden queasiness, her sudden sense of inferiority.

She turned to the second book. It had a cartoonish cover. It didn't make her insides clench in fear. She started to laugh. '*Dealing With People You Can't Stand: How To Bring Out the Best in People at Their Worst.*'

He grinned. 'I thought you'd get a kick out of that one.'

She hugged both books to her chest. 'Thank you.' His thoughtfulness touched her. 'That was really kind of you.'

He shrugged. 'You said you wanted to learn.'

'I do.'

They stared at each other for a long moment. If one of her friends had given her a gift, she'd hug them or kiss them on the cheek. She wasn't sure if she should kiss Dominic on the cheek. She wavered for a moment, but, just as she decided a quick peck couldn't hurt, Dominic snapped away. 'I have some emails I need to answer,' he said, heading for the dining table.

'It's, uh, my night to cook. I'll go rustle us up something to eat.' And she headed for the kitchen, still clutching the books to her chest.

CHAPTER SEVEN

BELLA shuffled into the living room on Sunday morning and came to a halt when she saw Dominic in his usual spot at the table, his head bent over a file that had to be at least a foot thick, before continuing on her way to the kitchen. Every other morning this week he'd already left for the hotel by the time she'd emerged.

He glanced up as she walked past and she thought he might smile, but with a nod he returned to his work.

She drank her first cup of coffee standing in the kitchen. The window over the sink afforded a glimpse of Newcastle harbour and in the morning light the water sparkled and glistened, the foam behind the ferry chugging across the harbour a frothy invitation. The sight of that sea spray made her restless, made her realise that while she'd been here a whole week the only part of the city she'd so far seen was the walk from the apartment to the hotel.

It was a nice walk, through a small park and up a short rise, and the view from the front of the hotel looking out over Newcastle beach was breathtaking, but she'd had enough of being cooped up. Being cooped up would not be conducive to creating the best restaurant the city had ever seen.

She glanced at the door. Nor the best hotel either, she suspected. Did Dominic mean to work for every minute of the entire two months they were here? Didn't he mean to take at least one day a week off to recharge his batteries and keep fresh?

She needed him relaxed before approaching him with her new budget proposal. She needed him fresh if he was to give that proposal a fair hearing. She needed him relaxed and fresh if she hoped to prove to him that she wasn't the spoiled brat he thought her.

She made toast and another cup of coffee and took it into the living room. She proffered her plate to Dominic on the way past, but he shook his head and continued to work. She perched on the edge of the sofa and, when she was sure Dominic's attention was completely immersed in his file, she fed Minky a corner of her toast. The cat even deigned to be petted for a few seconds before stalking away again.

That was a definite improvement. She stole a glance at Dominic. He ignored her as effectively as Minky now did.

She washed up her breakfast things, showered and dressed deliberately casually in jeans and a bright blue sweater, and when she came back out into the living room Dominic was still bent over that file. She planted her hands on her hips. 'You can't be serious, right?'

He glanced up and finally smiled, the blue of his eyes the same shade as the dancing water of the harbour she'd viewed earlier. It took her pulse off-guard, knocking it sideways and bumping up its speed. 'Good morning, Bella.'

She pulled in a breath. 'Good morning, Dominic.'

He set his pen down and leaned back in his seat. Somehow the dainty lines of the chair only served to emphasise his out-and-out masculinity. 'As I recall, you requested no cheerful chatter in the mornings, at least not until your second cup of coffee. How did I do?'

She gave in to the urge to smile back at him. 'Perfectly,' she had to admit. 'You were the epitome of the model housemate.'

'I aim to please.'

Ooh, she just bet he did.

'Now, tell me what I can't be serious about.'

She shook herself, and then stood awkwardly for a moment.

During the last week the table had become Dominic's territory and she didn't want to invade it, even when he gestured for her to take the seat opposite him. She propped herself against the arm of the sofa instead and tossed a tinkly ball for Minky, who ignored it.

Relaxed; she wanted him relaxed. And open. Friendly wouldn't hurt either. She straightened. 'Don't you believe in taking any time off?'

'This assignment is only for two months. I can rest when it's done.'

'Bzzz.' She made the sound of a game-show buzzer. 'That is so not the right answer.'

His lips twitched.

'I'm sorry, but you are not invincible, Mr Wright.'

'I'm not frightened by a bit of hard work, Bella.'

Neither was she, even if he didn't choose to believe that. Physically she'd worked harder in her uncle's restaurant—cooking, waitressing, washing dishes—than she had this past week, but there was no denying that this job was far more challenging. She lifted her chin. She'd prove to him yet how wrong he was about her. 'I know what you think of me, Dominic, but are you unhappy with the hours I've put in this week?'

'No, so far you're on track.'

She ignored the implicit scepticism stretching through his words. He didn't need to say it out loud—he didn't expect her to last the distance. Only time would prove to him how wrong he was.

'I happen to believe it's important to take time off. It keeps a body fresh and recharges the batteries.'

'Not everyone has that luxury, Bella.'

She rolled her eyes. 'Oh, *puh-leeze!* You aren't one of those poor sods, Dominic, so you can drop the "high and mighty martyr" act.'

He threw his head back and laughed. It bumped her pulse rate up again. She rolled her shoulders, vexed with herself for snapping at him, for letting him rile her and get under her skin. *Relaxed*, she ordered. *Fun, light, cheerful.*

'If you get sick because of overwork, you know who my father will blame, don't you?' She slapped a hand to her chest. 'Me! I refuse to be responsible for that.'

'I promise I'm not about to keel over and take sick.'

She eyed him a moment. 'You appreciate straight talking, right?'

'The straighter the better.'

'Okay, you're on notice— I will not let the effects of your overwork sabotage my restaurant.'

He pushed his chair back and twisted to face her more fully, his long legs stretched out in front of him and his expression intrigued. 'Would you care to explain that?'

She sent him her sweetest smile. 'I'd be delighted to. If you don't take any time off, if you work yourself into the ground, how do you expect to make the best business decisions? If you become over-tired your judgement will become impaired. Being as obsessive as you are, seemingly determined to work every single minute of every single day, is supposed to achieve what, exactly?' She didn't think that attitude would help to create the hotel her father had his heart set on.

Dominic folded his arms. He didn't answer.

'I think it's important for the person in charge to have, and display, some balance.'

His lips twitched again. 'You think I'm unbalanced?'

She opened her mouth to deliver something suitably crushing, and then she remembered the dispiriting blankness of his bedroom. And all those many, many conquests of his—none of whom had lasted beyond a couple of weeks. She also remembered she was supposed to be doing fun, light-hearted and cheerful so she rolled her eyes in mock-exasperation. 'You said it, buddy.'

A low rumble emerged from his chest. It made the breath jam in her throat. As soon as the sound had melted away, he jerked upright in his chair, his eyes hard and narrowed. 'Is this some roundabout way of asking me for time off, Bella? Because, let me tell you now, there's not a scarecrow's chance in hell of that happening.'

'It's me telling you up front that I have no intention of working on Sundays.'

He really did have the most appalling opinion of her, didn't he? They glared at each other for a moment. Then Dominic eased back into his seat. 'That seems fair enough. I'm sorry I jumped to conclusions.'

She had a feeling he wasn't the least bit sorry. Suddenly fun, light-hearted and cheerful all flew out of the window. She wasn't going to let him wreck her father's hotel. Dominic knew how to ruthlessly take over a company, and he knew what it took to increase efficiency and productivity. He knew how to wheel and deal, but did he know how to nurture a dream? Did he know how to grow something from its very beginnings?

'You're commitment-phobic in your personal life. Are you in business, as well?'

His head snapped back. 'Of course not!'

She slammed her hands to her hips. 'How much of your heart do you mean to give the hotel?'

He stared at her as if she'd just grown horns. 'It doesn't need my heart. It needs my business smarts.'

'This whole project—it's just a stepping stone for you, isn't it?'

'And for you.'

'I want this hotel to honour my mother and my father. But you, you just want results in the short-term. The long-term is someone else's problem as far as you're concerned, isn't it? You're not interested in creating a…a culture.'

'Bella, you're losing me.'

She tapped her foot. 'How much of this city have you seen?'

'About the same as you, I expect. Plus, I read the *Lonely Planet* piece.'

The publication had named Newcastle as one of the top ten cities to visit in 2011.

'And I've read all the tourist brochures.'

'You think that's enough?'

'I know what the city has to offer.'

'But you haven't experienced any of those offerings.'

'I don't need to.'

She leapt up from the arm of the sofa. 'Yes, you do!'

'Why?'

'So you can make sure that the Newcastle Maldini is the best!' She was starting to fear that the Newcastle Maldini wasn't going to be any different from the hundreds of other five-star hotels already in existence. That didn't seem fair to her father. And it didn't seem fair to Dominic who worked so hard either. 'Look, it's like Hamlet, right?'

He blinked. 'I'm a lot of things, Bella, but an indecisive Danish prince isn't one of them.'

She tried to gather her thoughts so she could explain them to him. 'It's the idea that if something is rotten in the state of Denmark—the idea that if the king is ineffectual or corrupt—then that filters down to the rest of the society.'

He scratched both hands back through his hair, making it stand on end. Bella had to fight the sudden urge to reach out and smooth it back down. 'Are you accusing me of being ineffectual or corrupt?'

'Oh, don't be ridiculous! But don't you see? At the hotel you're the equivalent of the king. Your attitude filters down through your managers and then to the rest of the staff.'

'So if there's something wrong in my attitude—?'

'Precisely. Now, I understand the emphasis on excellence in service and the luxuriousness and comfort of the hotel et cetera.' She cut in before he could start to get angry or offended. 'Of course that's the kind of reputation we want to foster.'

'But?'

'But don't you feel there's something missing?'

He leaned forward and stared at her intently. 'Like?'

She frowned, trying to find the words to verbalise a feeling, a sense of unease that was vague at best. 'What,' she started slowly, 'is going to make the Newcastle Maldini different from all the other Maldini hotels?'

'I don't want it to be different! I want all the Maldini hotels to share a reputation for excellence.'

She frowned harder and tried again. 'Okay, then what is going to make the Newcastle Maldini different from any of the other five-star hotels in the area? What is going to make someone decide to stay there rather than somewhere else?'

'I take it you do have an answer?'

'What about a working understanding of the city's diversity and all that it has to offer?'

He shifted impatiently. 'We have advertising and PR people who will take care of that. I know that you don't fully understand business, Bella, but the concierge and reception staff will be thoroughly versed in the cultural and leisure activities the city has to offer.'

'Oh, yes, they'll be thoroughly versed, but they'll take their cue from you.' Her hands clenched in sudden frustration. 'Don't you think we all need to experience the city, to develop a proper appreciation and understanding of it?'

He frowned at her again.

'Because,' she pushed on, 'what use will all that knowledge be? It'll simply be a soulless passing on of facts without enthusiasm or passion.'

'We'll be providing our patrons with information they request, that's what good it will do.'

'But we won't be offering them anything additional. We won't be giving them anything distinct or different from any other hotel.'

He folded his arms and leant back. She had no idea what he was thinking. Finally she shook her head. 'You really don't get it, do you?' The Maldini hotel had to have a heart and soul, a unique and distinctive spirit.

He stared back at her with hooded eyes. He didn't say anything. She thought back to his bedroom with its horrid blankness.

'Okay.' She clapped her hands. 'Come on, we're going out. I'll see if I can't show you what I mean.'

He stared down at his file and pursed his lips.

'Oh, please, Dominic, it's Sunday!'

'I'm not going to get any peace until I do, am I?'

'Very perceptive of you.'

He surrendered with a sigh.

By the time she'd checked Minky's water bowl and had topped up her cat biscuits, Dominic was ready. Bella shoved her keys into one pocket and some money in the other.

He nodded to the money. 'What's that for?'

'Ice-cream.'

'By eating ice-cream I'm going to experience the heart of Newcastle?'

She raised an eyebrow. 'Do you doubt it?'

He laughed and followed her to the lift. When they reached the street, he said, 'Did you have a particular destination in mind?'

'Oh, yes.' Without another word, she set off towards the hotel. Ignoring the staff entrance, she led him across the road until they stood opposite the beach. 'This view has been taunting me all week.'

'Taunting?' He followed her down to the boardwalk below. 'I've been enjoying it.'

Something niggled at her as she glanced back at him. It scuttled out of reach as she tried to grasp it.

The beach gleamed in the morning sun, the water glorious shades of blues and greens. It wasn't warm enough yet for swimming, but there were a handful of surfers catching the curling breakers that built up out the back, and children paddling along the shoreline and playing in the sand. Farther up the beach, a game of volleyball was underway. Bella dragged salt air into her lungs and her shoulders loosened. 'Well, I've enjoyed it, too,' she admitted. 'But I've been dying to be a part of it.' Hadn't he?

She had the sudden stomach-sinking sensation that Dominic's answer to that would be 'no.' She flicked a glance at him. Why not? He enjoyed...

She frowned. Actually, what precisely did Dominic enjoy? What had she *seen* him enjoy?

He seemed to enjoy joking with his staff. She bit her lip and recalled the lecture he'd given her about the importance of teamwork. Did he truly enjoy those jokes or was it simply part of a strategy—a charm offensive—to keep everyone motivated and happy?

Given his reputation, he must enjoy sex.

But it was sex without commitment. There was no long-term enjoyment to be had there.

Walking so close beside him that she could pull great swathes of his cinnamon scent into her lungs, it suddenly seemed seriously unwise to contemplate his sex life.

'Take a deep breath,' she ordered, setting off in the direction of the art deco façade of the ocean baths pavilion, and turning her face into the faint breeze so she dragged salt rather than cinnamon into her body. 'Isn't it heavenly?'

She rushed on before he could disoblige her by grunting out a 'no.' 'Did you have any beach holidays as a child?'

'No.'

That was grunted out with disobliging curtness. His face shuttered closed and she wondered what particular raw nerve she'd hit this time. Suddenly her reasons for wanting him relaxed and calm seemed trivial and petty; selfish. He worked so hard. He deserved some quality down time, with no hidden agendas. She suddenly wanted him to enjoy the day just for itself.

'Well, there's nothing stopping you from having beach holidays as an adult, is there? You can pretend you're on holidays today.'

Some of the tightness eased out of him. 'And why would I want to do that?'

'Because holidays are lovely. And...'

'And?'

'I'm pretending I'm on vacation today and the pretence will be easier to maintain if you play along.'

His grin hooked up one side of his mouth. Without even seeming to realise it, he lifted his face to the sun and ran one hand through his hair. Her breath caught at the sight of all of that red-gold firing to life in the sun. Her heart slammed against her ribs.

Oh, good Lord! She wrenched her gaze away before she did something daft like stumble into a pothole or crash into something solid and unmoveable.

They walked on in silence for a bit. Bella hoped it was a companionable silence, only she couldn't swear it was. She was too busy trying to get her slavering hormones back under control.

Deep breaths, Bella. Deep breaths.

The ocean baths gave way to a vast rock-shelf. At low tide the rock pools would sparkle in the sun and entice explorers. Bella made a mental note to check when the next low tide was due.

She pointed. 'Destination number one is up ahead. I've been dying to see the famous Nobby's Head with its celebrated lighthouse.' Nobby's beach spread along one side of the headland. The other side, complete with a breakwater, bordered the harbour.

'What's destination two?'

Something inside her loosened at his tone. It was no longer just amused tolerance or barely checked impatience. Something else had entered his voice—a hint of curiosity, perhaps?

'A stroll along the harbour foreshore.'

'Why?'

'There doesn't have to be a reason.'

'Yes, there does.'

'Because we're on holiday, then.'

Although he didn't say anything, she could tell he wasn't satisfied. She considered telling him the truth—that it was Sunday and she wanted to see how the people of Newcastle spent their Sunday—but that would only remind him of work. And suddenly work was the last thing on her mind.

She pulled him to a halt and pointed offshore. 'How many container ships can you count out there?'

He shaded his eyes and scanned the horizon. 'Twenty-two.'

'Twenty-two! And those are only the ones we can see. There'll be more back that way.' She gestured behind them. 'I'm hoping I get to watch at least one of them come into the harbour today. It's only a little harbour and they are big boats. I bet it's quite a show.'

Dominic stared at her for a moment and then threw his head back and laughed. 'Bella, you are such a child!'

But he said it so nicely she refused to take offence. And then they rounded the bend in the path and Bella found a brand-new beach stretching out in front of her—all the way to the headland with its lighthouse—and she couldn't resist its silent invitation. 'Ooh, look, it's glorious!' She raced down the steps to the beach, kicked off her shoes and dug her toes into the sand.

After a moment's hesitation, Dominic followed her. The sand was cool beneath his feet. He couldn't remember the last time he'd walked on a beach. He trailed behind Bella as she ambled along, seemingly aimlessly as far as he could tell, but it was no hardship watching her. Those snug jeans outlined her hips to perfection, and they had the most innocently sexy sway he could ever remember encountering.

Eventually she pointed farther up the beach. 'Let's go sit up there for a bit to soak all this up.'

He wasn't exactly sure what they were supposed to soak up, but he didn't argue. He was intrigued by whatever it was she was trying to prove to him today.

He was intrigued by the woman herself.

She threw herself down on the ground, the long strands of her hair touching the sand as she leant back on her hands and lifted her face skywards. She seemed at home here in a way she never was in their apartment. 'Did you have beach holidays a lot as a kid?' he found himself asking.

'Oh, yes, all the time when my mother was alive. We'd spend the summer holidays on the Sunshine Coast. It was idyllic.'

Her face came alive as she recalled those holidays and the ache to kiss her intensified. For the first time he felt a tiny tug of understanding for his father's weakness. The man had been a gullible sap, but—

But nothing!

He wrenched his gaze from Bella's face to stare out to sea.

'Did you go on holidays as a child, Dominic?'

His lips twisted. 'Holidays cost money, Bella, and there was never enough for the essentials when I was growing up, let alone extras like holidays.' He doubted that was something the pampered woman at his side would ever understand. Marco had shielded her from life's harsher realities.

'I'm sorry,' she murmured.

He didn't want her pity.

She hesitated. 'Was your childhood unhappy?'

He should have resented her probing. His normal tactic was to stonewall personal questions, but he'd started to realise that normal tactics didn't work where Bella was concerned. Maybe it had something to do with the fact they were sharing that God-awful apartment.

Maybe revealing the vast gulf that lay between them would serve as a reminder why kissing her would be such a disastrous idea. Maybe it would remind him that, although she had vivacity and an animation that called to him, she was still a woman—a woman who had continually taken advantage of her father's love and patience. She would do the same to any man.

But he wasn't a chump like his father, and he had no intention of ever becoming one.

'When my father lost his job and found it hard to get work again, my mother left him.' He met Bella's gaze head-on. 'I never saw her again.'

Her eyes widened. Her bottom lip quivered. 'She left you, too?'

His disclosure was meant to create a barrier between them. The softness warming her eyes shouldn't have him wanting to lay his head on her shoulder to rest for a while.

'Oh, Dominic, that's dreadful! How old were you?'

He shrugged, made his voice uncaring, though that was harder than it should've been. 'Nine.'

'How did your father deal with that?'

'Alcohol.'

His heart burned at her quick intake of breath. He could just imagine how shocking it must seem to her. 'He did have his sober periods when he picked up work and dangerous women.'

She swallowed. 'Dangerous?'

'No sooner did he get a new job then there'd be a new woman to spend all his money on.'

When he'd had it, Christopher Wright had thrown money around like there was no tomorrow, uncaring that there was next to no food in the house, that the electricity bill hadn't been paid, that his son needed new shoes and schoolbooks. As long as he'd had men slapping him on the back for buying the next round of drinks, and women batting their eyes at him, all had been right in Christopher's world. When Dominic had tried to remonstrate with him, he'd simply laughed it off and claimed that tomorrow would take care of itself.

'My father married and divorced another three times by the time I was sixteen.'

She gaped at him. 'Three?'

'All who took him to the cleaners in the divorce settlements. Not that he had much left in the end.' His father had lost heart after wife number four had deserted him. 'That's when he hit the bottle hard.' Luckily, Christopher had always been a jovial drunk.

Dominic's lips twisted and he gave one hard shake of his head. 'My father either couldn't make money or he couldn't hold on to it.' His father's eventual disillusion had burned itself on to Dominic's soul; the poor bloody schmuck. Dominic had never envied him his optimism for the future. He'd always known it would end in disappointment.

He'd been very careful never to cultivate that kind of optimism in himself.

He turned to her. 'Your father helped me with him, you know?'

Her brows shot up. 'He did? How?'

'My father developed alcoholic dementia and needed full-time care. Before I could move him into my apartment, he took off. I couldn't find him. Marco put multiple men on the case, looking for him. Eventually we discovered him washed up at a welfare centre.'

'I'm glad Papa could help.'

Dominic had barely been out of university. 'He then organised the best doctors to examine him.'

Not that it had made any difference. His father's alcoholism had been too far gone by then. Bella didn't know how lucky she was to have Marco for her father.

The resentment he'd felt for her that first day in Marco's office started to slip away. Bella may take her father for granted, but he was starting to see that it didn't mean that she didn't love him. It didn't mean that she was cold or hard or uncaring.

In fact he was starting to see that the exact opposite was true.

They were both silent for a long moment. Finally Bella said, 'He must've loved your mother very much.'

He stiffened. 'What makes you say that?'

'To spend so long trying to replace her.'

He didn't answer. It wasn't an idea that had occurred to him before. His hands clenched. It made no difference now, anyhow.

'It's a pity you couldn't all have gone on at least one beach holiday together.'

He didn't answer that either.

'Good memories like that can help.'

He doubted it.

She nudged his shoulder with hers and grinned. 'You want to know one of my father's favourite things to do at the beach?'

He stared back, his interest piqued. He found it hard to imagine Marco at the beach. 'What?'

She grabbed his hand, hauled him to his feet and then tugged him down towards the shoreline with its damper sand. 'He loves to build sandcastles.'

She dropped to her knees and started digging. It was so unexpected it startled a laugh from him.

'They weren't just any old sandcastles, mind.'

A gust of breeze tugged at his hair. She glanced up and grinned. He grinned back. 'Of course not, this is Marco we're talking about.'

'Exactly! We had moats and turrets and tunnels and interconnecting channels and… Oh, you name it! C'mon, chop-chop, you can get started on the moat and channel.'

Dominic hunkered down on his knees, pushed a hand into the sand and started digging, created a channel that led down to the water's edge. He felt ridiculously elated when a wave swept up the channel to fill their moat, and when Bella clapped her hands in glee.

They dug; they built a ridiculously elaborate system of buildings and walls within the boundary of the moat. He whistled; Bella hummed. He didn't know for how long they worked, but a squeal from Bella alerted him to an incoming rogue wave. He grabbed her hand and hauled her out of its path, his arm going around her waist to half lift her. Breathless and laughing, she grinned up at him.

The breath shot out of him. His grip on her tightened. She stilled. He could read the question in her eyes—was he going to kiss her?

Would she let him?

When she didn't move away, he had his answer.

Heat surged through him, the temptation pounding at him like the surf breaking on the reef. Bella would taste divine. He wanted to bury his face in her neck and inhale her, and then he wanted to capture her lips in his and devour her slowly, thoroughly. He wanted to memorise the curves of her body with his hands...

Icy water hitting his feet and ankles brought him back to earth and made Bella jump, breaking the spell.

'Oh, look.' She pointed to their sandcastle, now laid to waste by the wave.

His jaw dropped. All their hard work washed away as though it had never existed!

But Bella only laughed. 'That's the joy of sandcastles,' she confided, bumping shoulders with him again before moving away. He missed the feel of her so close—her vital heat, her soft curves.

'Joy?' It was all he could do to keep his voice steady.

'You can always start afresh tomorrow on an even more ambitious project.'

He shook his head, but her words lightened him.

Her face suddenly lit up. She tugged on his arm and hopped from one foot to the other. 'Look, look!'

It took all of his strength to look away from her face and to where she pointed, but when he did a laugh escaped him. A container ship was making its way towards the mouth of the harbour.

She let go of his arm and set off up the beach to where they'd left their shoes. 'Hurry up!' she called back over her shoulder. 'There's no way I'm missing this.'

He found himself breaking into a jog, unable to resist her enthusiasm. And, as he jogged after her, he couldn't help wondering how different his childhood might have been if his mother had had a bit more of Bella's spirit.

'So, what's your verdict on Newcastle?' Dominic asked when they let themselves back into their apartment, much later that day.

'Oh, I just love it!'

He rolled his shoulders, not comfortable with how easily she could bandy that word about.

She grimaced as she entered the apartment. She walked across the room and tried to tug the curtains a few inches wider, but the light continued to pool in a kind of sexy halo about the love seat, the table and the sofa. Airy brightness was not this apartment's selling point.

She turned, shrugged and waved an apologetic hand at the curtain almost as if to say, *You try*. But then she smiled. 'I had the best day.'

After the demolition of their sandcastle, they'd raced across to the harbour foreshore and had eaten takeaway fish and chips while watching the tugboats bring the container ship into berth. Bella's wide-eyed wonder had made him feel younger.

They'd strolled along the foreshore for a while, enjoying the sun and the breeze, and the way both brought the harbour to life, before retracing their steps and ambling through the throng of picnickers in the foreshore park. Then they'd bought ice-creams and sat on a park bench by the beach to eat them. Bella had regaled him with tales of holidays past.

It was early spring but it had felt like summer.

'What's *your* verdict of Newcastle?'

He frowned. She straightened from petting Minky to slam

her hands to her hips. 'Are you saying you didn't enjoy yourself today?'

He shook his head. 'It was fun.' Unexpected, but undeniably fun. That had been the biggest surprise of all.

'Then why the frown?'

'After the day we've had, I figured your question deserved a considered answer.'

'Oh.' She blinked. 'Okay.' She sat on the sofa and waited. She didn't try to hurry him.

'It's a place of contrasts,' he finally said. 'There is still a definite hangover from its industrial past.' Newcastle had once been a steel city; its vast steelworks had provided the city with much of its prosperity. Steam, smoke and fire had once lit up its skies, but the steelworks were long gone and the city had needed to reinvent itself. 'The beaches are beautiful and the harbour foreshore has been sympathetically reclaimed. Both are…nice places to be.'

She wrinkled her nose at the term 'nice'. He shook his head to tell her he wasn't done yet. 'The people are no-nonsense, but friendly. There's a blue-collar mentality and a cosmopolitan sophistication that somehow manage to coexist in harmony. I'm surprised,' he admitted. 'It's extraordinary.'

As he spoke, he strode back and forth in the space between the table and the sofa. He swung to her now. 'Is that what you wanted me to experience?' he demanded. She'd found him lacking in something earlier. Did she still?

'I just wanted you to see for yourself how unique this place is.'

Her answer didn't satisfy him, but he couldn't explain why.

She leaned towards him and for some reason it reminded him of that moment when he'd considered kissing her. His skin went tight.

'Tell me the truth. After today aren't you even more determined to make the Newcastle Maldini a success?'

He blinked. He considered her question. Damn it, yes!

Bella didn't press him for an answer. With a little shrug, she rose. 'I'm going to take a bath.'

'Bella?'

She turned in the doorway.

'Why don't you think I can make the hotel a success?'

Her chin shot up. 'I didn't say that you couldn't. I'm hoping very much that you can.'

'But what is it exactly that you don't think I have? What quality or qualities do you think I lack?'

'You really want to know?'

His gut clenched. He nodded.

She shifted her weight. 'What motivates you, Dominic?'

He thought for a moment. 'Pride.' Pride in his work. Pride for a job well done.

She shook her head. 'That's not what I think. I think you never want to be that little boy again, dependent on other people's whims and living a hand-to-mouth existence.'

He froze.

'You work as hard as you do so you never have to be in that situation again. I understand that, but you're not working towards something—you're simply trying to prevent history from repeating itself. When will you decide you have enough money and success? Or will you never have enough?'

She was wrong! She had to be wrong!

'Passion,' she finally said. 'That's what you don't have, Dominic. That's what you lack—passion.'

CHAPTER EIGHT

On Monday, Dominic saw the poster on the noticeboard in the staff lunchroom advertising Bella and Luigi's Bistro for Beginners—a complimentary cooking school for all Maldini hotel staff starting this Thursday evening. *All Welcome!*

On Thursday evening, Dominic pushed through the kitchen doors and then stopped dead when he saw how many staff members had shown up for Bella and Luigi's Bistro for Beginners. He started counting heads and stopped at twenty.

Were they all here for Bella's cooking school?

He shifted his weight from the balls of his feet to his heels. He'd been dubious as to how this idea of hers would fly. He'd shown up to boost numbers, totally unnecessary with this turn-out, he now saw.

He could sneak out again if he wanted and get back to all that paperwork waiting on his desk.

He shoved his hands in his pockets. He didn't make for the door. While her flyers and posters had promised fun, he suspected there was more behind this project of hers. She'd taken his lecture about team spirit to heart, it was more than that, too. She wanted to instil a passion in the staff for working at this hotel.

Because she didn't believe it was something he could accomplish.

So it'll just be like every other five-star hotel. Acid filled his mouth. He was starting to think she might have a point.

He'd avoided her for the majority of this week—ever since their day in the sun—but he hadn't been able to block her startling dissection of the motives that drove and rode him, of the reasons he worked so hard. She was right about them, too. It explained the restlessness and the lassitude that tried to settle over him whenever he began to slow down. He might not like what she had to say but, now he could see the truth in her words, he had no intention of ignoring them.

For all her faults, he'd bet Bella had never had to fight a dreariness of the soul. He wanted to discover her secret for keeping it at bay, for chasing it away. That was the real reason he was here tonight. If he wanted to learn her secrets, he had to stop avoiding her.

Bella turned from where she was conferring with Luigi and she clapped her hands to gain everyone's attention. Slowly the room came to order. 'First, I'd like to say how wonderful it is to see so many people here this evening and to welcome you all to our very first cooking club. At this point I want to stress—'

She broke off when she saw Dominic. For some stupid reason he found it hard not to fidget.

'Did you need me for something, Dominic?'

He shoved his hands deeper into his pockets. 'I, uh, I saw your poster in the lunchroom. I thought I'd come along and get some tips from a master.'

Her eyes widened. He didn't blame her for her surprise. He'd made sure they'd barely clapped eyes on each other this past week.

He swallowed. 'It did say *all* staff were welcome.'

She smiled and it made his gut clench. 'Of course you're welcome, Dominic. Now.' Her gaze travelled about the room again and he found he could breathe more freely. 'I want to stress that we are all equals here tonight, regardless of what position you hold within the hotel's hierarchy.'

That was a smart move. There was staff in here from housecleaning and reception; there were bar and waiting staff as well as a couple of managers. Even Luigi's brother-in-law had snuck in.

'Oh, except for Luigi and I, of course—we are the bosses.'

He could've sworn she'd twinkled that right at him. The titters and swift glances cast his way confirmed it. As always, her sassiness fired his blood.

'The purpose of the class is twofold. First and most importantly, it gives us a chance to get to know each other, hopefully while having fun. Secondly, it's to give you all the opportunity to benefit from the not inconsiderable experience and amazing talent of Luigi here—and *moi*.' She touched her hand to her chest and bowed her head in exaggerated false modesty, and a ripple of laughter travelled around the room.

A chuckle rumbled free from Dominic's chest, too. What was it about this woman? She held this small crowd in the palm of her hand and they hung on to her every word. If it were him up there, everyone would listen to him attentively because he was the boss, but he wouldn't engage them the way Bella had just done.

'If nothing else, you do at least get to take your dinner home with you tonight. Now, because I'm the boss—' she twinkled at Dominic and everyone laughed again '—I got to choose what we are cooking tonight, but there is a suggestion box in the lunchroom if anyone would like to put forward a recommendation for one of our upcoming cooking clubs. Indian cuisine is my favourite, so we're making a simple chicken madras curry. Are there any vegetarians here?'

Several people raised their hands.

'Don't worry, I haven't forgotten you. You'll be making a delicious pumpkin and chickpea curry.'

Dominic planted his hands on his hips and watched her closely. There was no doubt that she was enjoying herself.

'We'll be working in pairs, so I want you to choose a partner and move across to one of the workstations.'

A couple of female staff members flicked flirtatious glances his way. He ignored them, introduced himself to Matthew—a porter—and invited him to join him. They moved to a workstation at the back of the room.

Dominic told himself that, as boss, he wanted to keep a low profile and not let his presence interfere with Bella's class. But down here at the back he could also follow her every move without fear of being caught out.

He and Matt followed—or attempted to follow—Bella's instructions to chop the chicken into two-centimetre dice. Dominic dispelled Matt's awe by making a veritable mess of the chicken.

'I'll, uh, do the onions,' Matt volunteered, obviously getting in before Dominic could make a mess of those, too.

'Okay, now it's time to select the chillies,' Bella called out. 'For those of you who prefer a milder curry, take one of these banana chillies. If you like a little more heat take two of these jalapeno chillies.'

Dominic couldn't help himself. 'What if you like it really, really hot?'

Her lips twitched. Her caramel eyes, full of challenge, turned to him. 'Then you need two of these bird's eye chillies.'

It took more effort than it should to drag his eyes from the luscious temptation of her lips to the box she indicated. He swallowed. 'Do you like it hot, mate?' he asked Matt.

'You bet.'

He strode up to where Bella stood and grabbed a handful of bird's eye chillies. Bella laughed when she saw how many he had. He swore he could listen to that sound all evening. 'Uh, Dominic, you won't need that many. They are seriously potent.'

'Good.'

'I don't think—'

'They're not as big as those first ones you held up.' He wondered if he should take one of those, too. He loved a good curry. His mouth had already started to water in anticipation.

He hadn't managed anything more than a hurried sandwich at lunchtime, and that suddenly seemed like a long time ago.

The twitching of her lips became a full-blown smile that had the power to kick him in the guts, fire his blood to life and constrict his lungs all at the same time. 'Hasn't anyone ever told you that size doesn't matter?'

His lips lifted in a wicked grin of their own. 'Nope, no one's ever told me that before.'

Her eyes widened, her cheeks grew pink and then she laughed. His insides sat up and begged. This woman was ten times more potent than chillies. He had a feeling she was more potent than an unexploded bomb.

She nodded at the chillies. 'Well, on your own head be it.' Her eyes suddenly gleamed. 'Though I will advise you to discard the seeds. They hold the greatest heat.'

No way. He had no intention of wasting those.

With a wide smile she turned back to the rest of the class. 'Luigi will now show you the correct way to de-seed and chop your chillies.'

When all the pots were finally simmering on their individual hotplates, Bella and Luigi discussed the different ingredients that could be added or substituted to either the chicken or vegetarian recipes, and then they held a general question-and-answer session. Dominic couldn't believe how much he enjoyed the class.

Or how much he learned. A good curry was one of life's little pleasures, but he'd never tried to cook one before. He glanced across at his and Matt's pot and his chest puffed out. This cooking gig wasn't all that hard. He wondered if Bella would consider teaching them how to make lasagne next. He'd pop that into her suggestion box.

No matter what she intended to teach, he'd be here. She'd chosen exactly the right tone for the evening, and once word got around places in here would be seriously limited. Rather than pairs it'd be groups of four and six around workstations.

As far as a getting-to-know-you exercise went, it was ingenious. He should've thought of something like this himself. Different departments had held meet-and-greet sessions for their staff, but no one had thought to organise a hotel-wide one. No one except Bella, that was.

And Bella was the reason he'd enjoyed the class. Everything about her had his saliva glands kicking into overdrive. Her deft movements had mesmerised him as she'd demonstrated this technique or that. Her butter-rich voice as she'd moved about the room making suggestions here and there had melted him. Her passionate flourishes had parts of him burning harder and hotter than the curry simmering on the stove.

But it was her passion for food and cooking that had engaged them and fired them all with a similar enthusiasm.

Was it that simple? That Bella's zest for life was the result of engaging in the things she loved, such as cooking?

He loved his job, didn't he?

He shook his head. Not the way Bella loved cooking. She beamed and literally glowed in the kitchen when she was cooking. He recalled her rigid shoulders as she'd sorted through the vegetables the last time he'd been down here. He thought about the way she frowned over her files and laptop in the apartment, and it hit him that Bella didn't love the administrative side of being a restaurant manager the way she loved cooking.

His hands clenched. So what the hell was her secret?

Bella clapped her hands and claimed his attention again. A smile hovered on her luscious lips, tensing him up inside. 'Okay, everyone, turn off your hotplates.'

She was so full of…life! He'd ask her outright for her secret only he doubted she'd be able to answer him. She probably wouldn't have a clue what on earth he was talking about. It was something intrinsic to her nature—deep-seated and ingrained.

Matt leant across him to turn off their hotplate. Dominic shook himself and told himself to get with the programme.

Only Bella chose that precise moment to hit him with one of her mega-watt smiles. It froze him like a deer in the headlights.

'We have two more important lessons to take away with us today.'

Lessons, huh? As she moved towards him with that sensuous sway of her hips and the fullness of her breasts pressing against her chef's tunic, all he could think were the lessons he'd like to teach her: lessons of love. Blunt, unadulterated images blazed themselves on to his brain, ensuring he'd never get a decent night's sleep again.

She halted in front of him and her smile widened. He craved to reach out and trace the plump fullness of her bottom lip with his thumb. She reached under the bench behind him and everything inside him that had clamoured as she'd drawn near slammed to a halt when her shoulder brushed his hip.

She straightened again. He had to blink a couple of times to clear his vision. She held a plate. 'I'm going to ask Dominic to sample his curry.'

She spooned a small amount of meat and sauce onto the plate, handed it to him with a fork and then waited expectantly. He wondered why she'd chosen him. With a shrug, he did what she so obviously expected and shovelled the food into his mouth.

'Water won't help,' she said, *sottovoce.*

Wouldn't help what?

The curry hit the back of his throat. He doubled over and started to choke. If he'd had any breath left in his body he'd have yelled or groaned or something. His face started to burn and he swore it must have turned a deep red from the neck up. Perspiration broke out on his forehead and top lip. Tears started to stream from his eyes. 'I'm dying,' he finally managed to croak.

Bella ignored him to turn back to the rest of the class. 'Important lesson number one—always follow the recipe to the letter the first time you try it. Once you know how the original recipe tastes, then you can experiment and set about adding your own touches. Dominic and Matt used three times the recommended number of chillies. Would you like to sample the curry as well, Matt?'

The young porter took a hasty step back. 'No, thank you.'

'Water,' Dominic gasped out, still bent double.

'I told you, water wouldn't help.'

Dominic wondered if it'd be quicker to drop to the floor and die now. He'd have no mouth or throat lining tomorrow. He groaned as the curry hit his stomach. There went his stomach lining, too.

'Important lesson number two...'

He tried holding his breath in the hope it would ease the burning as Bella calmly ambled towards the industrial-sized refrigeration units at the other end of the room. Nope, that didn't work. He winced as he dragged in a breath that made his lungs catch fire.

'If you get chilli in a cut or accidentally touch your eyes after you've chopped one—or simply eaten too potent a dose...'

His head shot around.

'The best remedy is to rinse your cut or eyes with milk.'

He watched her pull a carton of milk from the fridge and slowly take down a glass, but he couldn't wait. He staggered forward, seized the carton and gulped down great mouthfuls, the relief immediate and exquisite.

'Or to drink it,' Bella laughed.

The class laughed with her but he didn't care. He kept guzzling cool, soothing milk.

'You'll make yourself sick,' she chided, *sottovoce* again.

He reluctantly let her prise the carton from his hands. He waited for the burning to start back up. It did, but when it came it was merely a shadow of its former self and he slumped in relief.

Then he straightened, glared at her and pointed towards his and Matt's pot. 'That stuff is lethal! It's—'

'But I thought you liked it really, *really* hot.'

She raised an eyebrow and his collar tightened about his throat. She had tried to warn him, he acknowledged as she hip-swayed away.

'Okay, everyone.' She clapped her hands. 'You'll find containers over here. Matt, you can take your portion from my and Luigi's pot.'

She didn't make the same offer to him, but he had a feeling she knew it'd be a while before he could face another curry with any equanimity.

'That was a dirty, rotten trick!'

Bella nearly jumped out of her skin as Dominic barged into the apartment. Minky, who had been sitting on the sofa beside her, yowled and shot under the dining table. Bella's heart surged against the walls of her ribs. It didn't slow again when she saw that Dominic was grinning rather than scowling. In fact, that only made it thud harder. 'I, uh...' She couldn't seem to get her tongue to work properly.

'And I acknowledge it was entirely my own fault.' He grinned at her. 'But I should've realised how you were playing me.'

Yep, he should've.

He set his briefcase on the dining table. Minky peered out at him. Her tail still swished but her gaze had lost its narrow-eyed spite. It was as close to hero worship as the cat could manage. Bella sympathised with her wholeheartedly.

'Dumb cat,' Dominic muttered.

That made Bella grin. 'Don't give me "dumb cat". I'm on to you, Dominic Wright. You're the only one who could possibly have bought this wind-up mouse for said *dumb cat*.'

'This from the woman who cooks the *dumb cat* a piece of diced fillet steak every evening.'

How on earth did he know about that? She shook herself to say, 'Well, I'm very glad you've taken to the *dumb cat*, because

Mel rang earlier and she's been delayed. We may end up with Minky for the entire two months.'

He scowled and rolled his shoulders. It made her grin. His unexpected kindness to the cantankerous moggy made her want to hug him. Which would be a seriously bad idea, so she wound up the silly toy and set it on the ground instead. Right on cue, Minky emerged and preceded to dance around the mechanical mouse with her back arched, batting it occasionally with her paw. When it wound down she walked over to Dominic and meowed plaintively until he reached over to set the mouse going again.

It shouldn't turn a girl to mush. It shouldn't.

She gulped and did what she could to stiffen her spine when he walked over and planted himself against the arm of the sofa.

He rubbed his jaw. 'I wanted to tell you that your cooking class tonight was brilliant. It was an inspired idea. Well done, Bella.'

She stared at him. Warmth flooded her. 'Really?'

'You made it fun. The staff, they're going to love working for the Maldini with programmes like that in place.'

Her chin lifted. Her shoulders went back.

'And, what's more, you've inspired me.'

She had? She leaned forward. 'How?' And then she remembered the small dimensions of the sofa and eased back before his cinnamon scent could completely undo her.

'I've been thinking about the things you said to me last Sunday.'

She grimaced. She'd wanted to apologise for that all week, only there hadn't been an opportunity because Dominic was never here, or the time hadn't seemed quite right because Dominic always steered the conversation. 'I want to apologise about that, Dominic. I had no right to say those things.'

He waved her apology away. She couldn't discern an ounce of resentment in the holiday-blue of his eyes. 'I'm starting to see what you mean about defining what will make our hotel unique.'

Our? The way he said it did unnerving things to her. So unnerving she leapt up to shush Minky's meowing and wind her toy mouse up again. When she returned to the sofa she sat as far away from him as she could.

'I do know that's part of what you're trying to achieve with the cooking club. If the staff love working at the Maldini, then that will be silently communicated to our patrons.'

She hoped so, but it was such a small initiative. It wouldn't reach all the staff.

'You want the staff to be invested in the hotel. You want them to be as happy as you are to be working there.'

'You know what I hope for? I want a waiting list of potential staff who are dying to work for the Maldini hotel. I want staff queuing at the door vying for positions that become vacant. I want the hotel to inspire people to choose hospitality as their career of choice. Can you imagine it?'

He stared at her.

'And can you imagine staying in a hotel that the staff love and respect and are so proud to be a part of?'

'It's a seductive vision,' he finally said.

Had it seduced him?

'Like I said, Bella, you've inspired me. Because tonight was such a hit, it got me thinking.'

'About?'

'Do you think day excursions would be well received by the staff? Do you think they would enjoy them?'

Her jaw dropped. She hauled it back up into place. 'Yes!'

He grinned. 'Good, because I thought, if you weren't busy over the weekend, we could explore some options.'

'Ooh, that's an excellent plan. But in the meantime...' She leapt up and raced out of the room. She came back with a handful of brochures and held them up for him to see. 'I made a trip to the tourist information centre during the week.'

She crouched in front of the coffee table and started to spread them out. He knelt down beside her to see. 'I'm amazed,' she continued, 'at how much there is to see and do in Newcastle.'

'Like?'

She held a brochure out to him.

'Sand-boarding on Stockton sand dunes?'

'Stockton Beach is on the northern side of the harbour. It goes on for…oh, I don't know…miles and miles, and some of the sand dunes are thirty metres tall.' She pointed to the picture of the beach on the front of the brochure and then opened it up. Her hand accidentally brushed against his and the brochure wobbled dangerously. She set it on the table and pulled her hands back, did what she could to dispel the darts of awareness that coursed through her. 'See? They have the most amazing sand dunes.'

'The guys would love this,' Dominic breathed.

'So would the girls.'

His eyes rested on her for a long moment. It made things inside her heat up. 'I, uh… And there's a fabulous cruise up-river to the historic town of Morpeth which sounds like fun, too.'

But Dominic didn't glance at the brochure she held out to him. He pursed his lips and continued to survey her. Eventually she couldn't stand it any longer. 'What?' She found it impossible to keep the defensiveness out of her voice.

He shook himself. 'Sorry. I was just wondering…'

'What?'

He settled his back against the sofa, legs stretched out in front of him. His broad shoulders against the dainty lines of the sofa made a compelling image.

She swallowed. Good Lord! Was everything in this apartment designed to make her think about sex? 'What were you wondering about?'

'Why this hotel means so much to you. I know you want

your father to love the hotel, I know you want it to be a fitting tribute to your mother, but I can't help feeling there's more.'

'Oh.' She stared down at her hands.

'You don't have to tell me, of course. I was just wondering, that's all.'

His voice was gentle. She remembered how he'd built sand-castles with her last Sunday and found she didn't have the heart to deny him an answer. 'I'm a bit ashamed.' She glanced up. 'And I'm afraid you won't think well of me.'

Or, she amended silently, that he would think even worse of her.

'Try me.'

She sat back on her heels. 'The hotel's success is so important to me because I want to make Papa proud of me.'

'Bella, your father adores you.'

'He loves me, yes, but it is not the same as making him proud of me. I've only recently realised how my inability to settle on a career has disappointed him—hurt him, even.'

'Bella, I—'

'No, please don't make excuses for me or for him. I know for a fact that he blames himself for indulging me too much after Mama died.'

Dominic dragged a hand back through his hair.

'You see, Mama was the glue that bound us together. Papa and I are so very alike—both fiery and stubborn—but Mama was calm and serene and she kept us on an even keel.'

'Fifteen must've been a difficult age to lose your mother.'

She glanced up. 'I think nine would've been worse.' Dominic had lost his mother so young. At least she'd had another six years of wonderful memories to store up before her mother had been snatched away.

'We're talking about you,' he reminded her. 'Not me.'

He smiled and some of the heaviness left her. 'It took me a long time to get over her death. I'd never realised how much she helped me to find my way until she wasn't there any more.'

'So.' He frowned as if reassessing something. 'You lost your way?'

'Big time,' she sighed. 'After school I bounced around from one thing to the next, but nothing seemed to stick.'

'What changed?'

'My aunt and uncle in Italy took me in hand and set me to work in their restaurant.'

'And you found that you liked it?'

'I loved it! But when I returned home I found that Papa no longer had any faith in me.'

'That's not true.'

'Yes, it is, and it's my own fault. But the solution is in my own hands, too.' Determination gelled inside her. She straightened her spine, pushed her shoulders back. 'If I can show him what a great job I can do with the hotel restaurant, then he'll realise that I can be an asset to his company and then he'll be proud of me. That's why the hotel's success is so important to me, Dominic. My father is a good man. My inadequacies are not his fault. I don't want him blaming himself for them any more.'

Dominic's eyes had turned a deep, dark blue. He shifted and leaned towards her. 'I don't think you are inadequate, Bella.'

He meant it. She could see the sincerity in the line of his mouth and in the way he continued to hold her gaze. It brought her absurdly close to tears. 'Thank you,' she whispered.

'I know I've been hard on you. Unfairly so, I suspect.' He leaned closer and brushed a strand of hair back behind her ear. Her breath hitched. His hand lingered against her cheek. 'I don't think you will be able to help but make Marco proud of you.'

His faith in her meant a lot, but suddenly it wasn't her father she had on her mind any more. All she could focus on was the warmth of Dominic's hand curving against her cheek, the firm promise of lips that hovered tantalisingly near and the scent of cinnamon that dredged her senses. The ridiculous chandelier overhead steeped them in a pale pink light, bathing the man no more than a kiss-distance away in a red-gold halo. Temptation, that was what this man personified, and she wanted a taste.

'You better stop looking at me like that, Bella.' The hand belied his warning as it trailed a path down her cheek, her throat and then around to the back of her neck.

'Like what?' she murmured as his fingers moved back and forth across her nape, raising gooseflesh. She'd do whatever he asked when he touched her like that.

'Like you want me to kiss you.'

She dragged her gaze from the delicious promise of his mouth and back to his eyes. 'If you can tell me how to do that—' her voice came out all breathy '—I'll do my best to comply.'

He traced her bottom lip with the thumb of his free hand, sensitising the tender skin there, until with a gasp her lips parted.

'That's not how to do it,' he said, his voice low, his chest starting to rise and fall to the same tempo as hers. She moistened her lips and hunger flared across his face. 'Neither is that.'

Her pulse pounded in her ears. She stared at his mouth and knew she'd taste heaven if he kissed her. Both of his hands tightened on her face as she lifted her gaze back to his. 'You should draw away.' He swallowed. 'You should frown, flash scorn from those beautiful eyes of yours and press your lips together. You should—'

'No.' She shook her head. She should stay here and beg him with her body to kiss her until he gave her what she craved.

'Bella...'

'Dominic, please,' she whispered, her hands lifting to tangle in the silky strands of his hair and to pull him down to her aching, starving mouth.

With a groan, he tilted her head back and his lips claimed hers.

CHAPTER NINE

DOMINIC'S kiss devastated her. It stole her breath and it stole her mind. It left her clinging to him and drowning in an ocean of sensation.

As his lips plundered hers, pleasured hers, she came to life. His heat, his passion, became her heat and her passion. She'd known instinctively that he'd taste delicious, but she hadn't known that his kiss would encompass everything rich, divine and addictive. He tasted better than the most extravagant three-course meal she'd ever had. He tasted better even than the twelve-course degustation menu she'd once sampled.

He tasted better than chocolate mud cake.

As she found her balance again, she half lay across his lap and she tasted him as thoroughly and completely as he had her, attempting to define and name his very essence, to stamp it on her memory and her soul.

A groan broke from him and he wrenched his mouth from hers but, as the realisation filtered into her fogged mind that she must be crushing him with her less-than-lightweight body, he proceeded to press kisses against her neck that made her bones weak and her blood dizzy with need. She sagged against him.

His hands travelled down her body, curving around her hips to haul her closer. 'You are divine,' he murmured, his teeth gently tugging on the soft lobe of her ear. 'You have driven me wild from the first moment I saw you.'

She pulled back, but his eyes showed no guile, only the heat of passion. 'I'm—I'm too curvy,' she hiccupped.

'You're perfect,' he growled, then groaned when she slid one hand in between the buttons of his shirt to caress the hot skin of his chest.

He twined her hair around his hand, tugged her mouth back down to his and she fell into him.

Bella didn't know how much time passed. All she was aware of was lying full-length beside Dominic, lost at sea, drunk on his kisses. And then a sharp pain made her gasp.

Dominic swore. They shot upright, both clutching adjacent legs. Not too far away Minky glared and swished her tail. She batted her toy mouse and meowed.

'The rotten cat attacked us!' Bella glared back at Minky. 'I swear, I don't know how Mel puts up with you.'

'Yeah, well, the rotten cat has more sense than either of us.'

Her heart sank at the cold hardness that had crept into Dominic's voice. Without looking at him, she adjusted her clothes and then moved away. She couldn't prevent herself from desperately hoping he'd pull her back into the circle of his arms again and whisper reassurance into her ear.

He didn't.

Of course he wouldn't.

She took one look at his face and scooted right away from him, banging an elbow against the coffee table as she leapt to her feet. He shot a hand out to steady her but she batted it away and retreated to her love seat on the other side of the room. With a curse, Dominic shot to his feet and stalked over to the dining table.

She folded her arms, swallowed back the lump in her throat and finally dared to look him full in the face. 'That—' she waved a hand to the space between the sofa and coffee table, the space where they'd sprawled out full-length, kissing '—may well have been a mistake.'

'There's no two ways about it. It was undeniably a mistake.'

'But is it really necessary for you to now look at me as if I'm poison?'

He scratched a hand back through his hair and eyed her warily. 'For God's sake, Bella, you're a bloody virgin!'

'What's that supposed to mean?' She surveyed him for a moment and then leapt up, shaking. 'Oh, for pity's sake, I have an intact hymen—it doesn't mean I've had a frontal lobotomy! We kissed. Big deal. It sure as heck doesn't mean I've started to plan the wedding.'

He couldn't seriously believe she was gullible enough to read anything into that kiss, surely? She blew out a breath and hoped her stunned disbelief was written all over her face. 'We kissed, but it doesn't change anything. I still know you're a commitment-phobic freak.'

He leapt to his feet, too. 'Just because I don't want to get married, that doesn't make me a freak!'

'And being a virgin doesn't make me one either!'

He stared at her for a moment, scratched a hand back through his hair and then nodded. 'Point taken.'

And then there was silence, an awful, nerve-shredding silence. All Bella could think of was what she and Dominic could be doing right at that very moment if Minky wasn't the devil's own cat. She knew she should pick the cat up and hug her, thank her, but a treacherous, untrustworthy part of her wished they hadn't been interrupted and that right now they were…

She snapped the thought off and glanced at Dominic. He was staring at the spot where they'd kissed and she could see the same thoughts spinning through his mind. The same hungry 'what if?'

Argh! 'Coffee!'

Dominic jumped and shook himself. 'Good idea.'

He held the kitchen door open for her and touched a hand to the small of her back as she eased past. She jumped and then rounded on him. 'No touching!'

A slow grin hooked up one side of his mouth. 'Why, Bella…'

The rest of his sentence choked off when Bella reached up

a hand to cup his face. 'Are you saying I'm the only one that touching affects?'

He reached up and pulled her hand from his face, pushed it back down to her side and then let it go as if it burned him. 'No,' he ground out.

'Then no touching,' she ground back. She took a step away. 'It'll be safer that way. I have no desire to tease you, Dominic. Do you mean to—?'

'No!' He broke in before she could finish.

Who was she trying to kid? His very presence teased her, taunted her, filled her with longing. 'I don't know what to call it, but there's a *thing* between us.'

'Chemistry?'

'Exactly.' She swallowed. 'And it seems foolhardy to...to...'

'Test its limits?'

'Yes. Especially as there's an element of the forbidden that makes it all the more...'

She glanced up at him, waiting for him to supply an appropriate word. He shrugged instead.

'Intense,' she supplied for herself.

'Forbidden?'

Coffee; she was supposed to be making coffee. It'd be easier talking about forbidden things if she didn't have to look at Dominic while she was doing it. 'You're my boss. I'm your boss's daughter.'

'Complicated,' he agreed.

She ground coffee beans; the scent filled the kitchen. 'And I have no intention of sleeping my way to the top. This job is important to me, but it's not *that* important.'

He folded his arms and leant a hip against a kitchen bench on the other side of the room. 'I would never let sex interfere with any business decision I made.'

'Puh-leeze.' She mirrored his position and rolled her eyes. 'Are you saying that if we were sleeping together, and I threatened to withhold sex until I got my way on something, that wouldn't influence you?' She snorted in disbelief.

'If you threatened to withhold sex to try to win some concession in the workplace, I would do my damnedest to make you change your mind. I would set out to seduce you and I'd play dirty.'

They stared at each other, both breathing fast. Images hit her hot and hard. Somewhere along the way they'd edged closer together. They sprang apart. 'Well, it's a moot point,' Bella choked out.

'You have to stop saying stuff like that—*if we were sleeping together*. Hell! It's—'

'You're right,' she broke in, not wanting him to spell it out. 'Here.' She pushed a mug of coffee towards him.

'Thanks.'

Neither one of them moved. The kitchen with its cold, clinical lines seemed the safest room in the apartment. Unlike the rest of the apartment, its form was purely functional.

'Why are you a virgin, anyway?'

She had to close her eyes against the frustration that stretched through his voice.

'Sorry,' he ground out a moment later.

She nursed her mug between both hands. She couldn't look at him; he was just too tempting. 'If I told you why, you'd only scoff.'

He set his mug down and bent at the waist to rest his hands on his knees. He straightened. 'I promise not to scoff.'

She stared at him and then shrugged. Fine. She was about to plant some seriously scary pictures in his mind, which would probably be for the best. She slid up to sit on the bench; he did the same on the bench opposite.

'I'm thinking it's not because you haven't had the opportunity.'

She laughed at his wry tone and the knowing twist to his mouth. 'No, Marco hasn't kept me locked in either a convent or an ivory tower.'

The blue of Dominic's eyes sparked. 'I suspect he knows that would've had the opposite effect.'

That made her laugh too, because she suspected he might be right. He didn't say anything more while she gathered her thoughts and, unlike the silence that had descended around them in the living room, this one didn't prickle and burn. She was grateful for that.

'Unlike you, Dominic,' she finally said, 'I had the best role models for love and marriage that a person could have. Mama and Papa loved each other deeply. They adored one another.' She glanced across at him and his eyes reflected the night-lights outside the window. 'It was…nice. And I always knew that eventually that's what I wanted, too.'

He pursed his lips. 'How old are you—twenty-five?' At her nod he continued. 'Are you trying to tell me that in twenty-five years you have never considered yourself in love?'

'It's true. I haven't.' He blinked and she hitched up her chin. 'Have you?'

'Well, no, but I've never believed in love.'

'Oh, Dominic.' She shook her head sadly. 'My life would be so dreary and grey if I believed love didn't exist.'

His head snapped back. She gulped. 'Not that I'm saying your point of view isn't valid. It's just…' She swallowed. 'It's just not for me.'

'That was always taken as a given, Bella.'

But his voice was hard and she found she had to swallow again. 'I spent a lot of time with my mother towards the end. Because we knew she was going to die we had the opportunity to say things we may not have had a chance to say if circumstances had been different. Losing her was terribly hard, but I have some wonderful memories of her from that time.'

'Did your mother make you promise to save yourself for marriage?'

She stared at him in shock and then threw her head back and laughed. 'You obviously think my parents terribly medieval. I think that would've had much the same effect as Marco's ivory tower, don't you?'

He sat back.

110 BELLA'S IMPOSSIBLE BOSS

'We did talk about sex, though. She wanted me to keep safe and avoid an unplanned pregnancy. She made me promise to practise safe sex, but nothing more.'

'So, why?' He lifted his hands in the air.

She was quiet for a moment. 'One day we were just reminiscing and she told me how happy she and Papa had always been.' She glanced up. 'Did you know they met here in Newcastle?'

He shook his head.

'That's why Papa wanted to open the first Maldini hotel here. Mama was working as a nurse. Papa came here for business. She ran into him on her bicycle.'

He grinned. 'No doubt her nursing skills came in handy.'

'Papa always said he fell for her then and there.' Bella grinned. 'But Mama said that was nonsense and that he'd just hit his head too hard.'

He laughed. 'I like the sound of her.'

Bella wondered what her mother would've made of Dominic. She'd probably have liked him; he'd have made her laugh. But given his reputation she wouldn't have wanted him for her daughter.

Bella swallowed. She didn't want him either.

Liar.

She forced her mind back to the conversation. 'Mama told me that Papa was the only man she'd ever been with. And her face when she said that...'

'What?'

He leaned forward, his eyes intense and intrigued. Bella shrugged. 'She just looked so happy. And grateful. And...and happy.' She couldn't think of a more honest way to describe it. She would never forget that look. 'I don't care how lame that sounds, that's how it was.'

He frowned. 'And?'

He hadn't moved. She told herself they had a kitchen's width of distance between them. 'And I knew then and there.'

'What?'

'That that's what I wanted for myself. I want a true and lasting love like the one my parents had. I'm prepared to wait to get it. I expect in some instances love can't and shouldn't be rushed. In the meantime, though, I don't want to waste my time experimenting with shallow love affairs. I'm not interested in taking part in a string of meaningless encounters.'

His jaw dropped. 'How do you know they'll be meaningless unless you try?'

'If a man won't wait until I'm ready, then I figure he wasn't worth my time in the first place.'

'That's true, but don't you have to kiss a lot of frogs before you find the prince?'

'Kiss, not jump into bed with.' She folded her arms and frowned. 'Besides, love isn't something you have to practise for.'

'But what if you marry someone and then discover the sex is awful?'

She rolled her eyes. 'I'm guessing this isn't the time to point out that there's more to marriage than sex.'

He thrust out his jaw. 'Sex is important.'

'Okay, fine. You and me—we aren't going to, but if we did make love do you doubt that it'd be satisfying?' Because there wasn't a single doubt in her mind.

'No,' he growled out.

'Then I'm hoping that'll be the same when I finally meet my prince.'

'And in the meantime you'll be missing out on...'

'What?' she snapped. 'What exactly do you get out of all your bed hopping?'

'Pleasure,' he snapped back.

'And what about the awkwardness afterwards? The vague sense of dissatisfaction? The guilt? Maybe you don't feel those things, but I'm pretty sure I would. Pleasure, pah!' She smacked the air. 'I get pleasure from a good red wine, from chocolate mud cake, from a steamy, scented bubble bath, and none of those things leave me feeling awkward, dissatisfied or guilty.'

That wasn't a hundred per cent true; she might feel a bit guilty if she overdid it on the chocolate mud cake. 'Besides—' she suddenly rounded on him '—a woman can pleasure herself, you know?'

Dominic stilled. Bella's cheeks flamed. She couldn't believe she'd said that out loud. She couldn't look him in the face. Burying her head in her hands, though, wouldn't do any good. 'You said you wouldn't scoff,' she finally choked out.

He raised both hands in surrender. 'I'm not scoffing, I swear. But, Bella, don't you think you've put your parents' relationship on an impossibly high pedestal?'

'High, yes,' she acknowledged. 'But not impossibly so.'

He folded his arms and his eyes suddenly narrowed. 'Are you sure you don't use your virginity as a kind of weapon, or as a shield?'

'A shield?'

'To stop a man from getting too close.'

'Of course not! Why on earth would I do that?'

'We all have secrets, Bella, insecurities. Loving someone means sharing those things.'

Her mouth went dry.

'Of course, it could simply be a sign of immaturity.'

Her chin shot up. 'That is such a male thing to say! Having sex does not equate to being an adult.'

'Being an adult means knowing right from wrong, and knowing your own worth. It's not about pleasing other people. You want to please your father, Bella, but at what cost to your own identity? Besides, being adult means knowing the difference between reality and fantasy. From where I'm sitting, I'm not thinking you have a great grasp of the former.'

'What on—?' She gaped at him and then saw his game. This time it was she who folded her arms. 'You're just trying to deflect attention from yourself. You're right, sex is important. It means something. Or, at least, it should. That's why virgins like me scare the living daylights out of men like you—our expectations, our rosy view of love. It's why you never spend longer than a week in the same woman's bed, because you want to stop the sex from meaning something. Running away from the truth won't change it, though.'

They stared at each other for a long moment. Dominic finally shrugged. 'That's something I think we'll have to agree to disagree on.'

Her shoulders suddenly sagged. 'For heaven's sake, Dominic, don't you get tired?'

He didn't say anything. She couldn't read his face. She shook her head. 'Chalk and cheese,' she murmured. 'That's what we are.'

'Oil and water,' he agreed.

'I'm starting to wonder if we belong to the same species.'

He laughed. She leapt down from the bench before the sound could beguile her completely. 'Chocolate mud cake?'

'Excellent suggestion.'

Dominic muttered an imprecation under his breath when a key rattled in the apartment door. Damn. He'd meant to be long gone before Bella arrived home for the day. He turned his laptop off and shoved it into its bag.

He'd taken to working late and eating a takeaway in his office, not returning to the apartment until Bella would be in bed. With her door firmly closed. And hopefully bolted.

He hated this damned apartment. Living in it for over three weeks had not succeeded in reconciling him to cherubs, love seats or gilt furniture.

He clenched a fist. Over three weeks of having to resist the temptation of Bella!

He turned as she tripped into the room. She pulled up short when she saw him. 'Hey.' She tried a smile but it didn't reach her eyes. She lowered her handbag and briefcase to the coffee table. 'How's it going?'

He tried to match her casual tone. 'Hey, yourself. How's it going with you?'

'Good. Luigi and I have just had a conference with the linen suppliers, and also the furniture factory who are outfitting the dining room.' She twisted her hands together. 'Actually, I'm glad you're here. There's something I've been meaning to talk to you about.'

He twisted more fully around on his chair. 'What's that?'

'I...' Then she glanced around and frowned. 'Where's Minky? Normally she starts meowing at me the moment I get in.'

'Probably plotting some dastardly form of revenge for being cooped up in here all day.'

Bella peered under the coffee table and then behind the television unit. She pointed to the dining table. 'Is she under there?'

He looked. 'No.'

'Not hiding on one of the chairs?'

He checked again. 'Nope.'

'Just give me a moment...'

He turned back to his file, pretending to be immersed in it, but he was aware of Bella's every movement. She thoroughly checked the living room and then the kitchen. He listened to her soft footfalls as she moved down the hall to the bathroom. It was the only room left. Both he and Bella kept their bedroom doors very firmly shut; it seemed the wisest course of action somehow.

She raced back into the kitchen and emerged with a box of cat treats. She shook the box. 'Minky?' Shake, shake. 'Minky?' More shaking, but no Minky appeared.

'Aha!' Bella pounced on the wind-up toy mouse. 'If this won't bring her out of hiding then nothing will.'

He gave up pretending to work. They both waited until the toy had wound down. She turned wide alarmed eyes to his. 'Go check your bedroom,' she ordered, jumping up to check his.

He checked the room completely. No Minky.

He met Bella back in the hallway. Her face told him she hadn't had any luck either. At the shake of his head she pressed a hand to her stomach and turned green. 'Don't look like that,' he ordered, starting to feel alarmed. 'Damn cat has to be about here some place.'

He stalked back out to the living room, checked behind every curtain and every piece of furniture, and then under it. Twice. He even pulled the cushions off the sofa. He glanced at Bella and bit back a curse. He'd throttle the damn cat once he got hold of it for making Bella look so sick. She played with the rotten thing, fed it, petted it, did everything she could to make friends with it. Didn't it know how lucky it was?

He checked the kitchen cupboards, all of them. Bella, who had been blindly following him, reached across to open the dishwasher. 'Bella, the cat is hardly going to—'

'Empty.'

'Yeah, but—'

'It was full this morning. I loaded it before I went to work. This is a *serviced* apartment.' She turned and raced back down to the bathroom. 'Freshly laundered towels.' She held them up for him to see. 'The apartment was serviced *today.*'

Then he saw exactly what she meant.

'What if Minky escaped when the cleaner came in?'

He had a feeling he'd turned green, too. That pampered piece of fluff on the streets? Minky didn't stand a chance.

He could tell the exact moment she read that thought in his face. 'Bella, wait!' he hollered as she dashed for the door. He tried to grab her, but his mobile rang and the temporary distraction gave her all the leverage she needed. 'Wright,' he spat into it, flying out of the apartment after her.

The line crackled. 'What the blazes do you and Bella think you are doing?' Marco yelled down the line.

Dominic had no idea what he and Bella were supposed to have done and, frankly, at the moment he didn't care.

'Bad timing, Marco. I'll call you back.' He stuffed the phone in his pocket and took the fire escape stairs two at a time.

Bella could sure move when she wanted to. He had a sudden image of how she'd react if she found a squashed Minky on the side of the road and his feet grew wings. He burst out of the building, narrowly avoiding knocking over an entire family, and tracked Bella to the side alley where, practically on hands and knees, she was calling the cat's name.

A homeless guy sat beside a bin. Dominic approached in time to hear him say, 'You lookin' for a cat, miss?'

She swung to him. Dominic winced at her eagerness.

'Yes!' She raced over. 'Have you seen one? Where? Where did you see her?'

He shuffled upright. 'What's it worth to you?'

A sound midway between a choke and a shriek escaped Bella's throat. She seized the guy by the lapels of his shabby jacket. 'Tell me about the cat.' She shook him. 'Or so help me God—'

Whoa! Dominic pulled her back before the homeless guy's eyes bulged clean out of their sockets. He kept one arm firmly around her. 'Have you seen the cat?' he asked, fishing a twenty-dollar bill from his pocket.

The man glanced hungrily at the money, then at Dominic and finally at Bella. His shoulders slumped. 'Don't know nothing about no cat.'

Bella stiffened. 'Then why—?'

'Wasn't hard to figure out,' he muttered, unable to meet either Bella or Dominic's eyes. 'You were either looking for a dog or a cat. I figured nobody in their right mind would call a dog Minky.'

Bella's shoulders slumped. Dominic wrestled with anger that the guy had upset her, and pity at his miserable condition. Pity won out. With a sigh he stuffed the twenty dollars into the guy's top pocket.

'Oh, God, Dominic.'

Bella's eyes filled and Dominic's gut clenched. He had to make this right for her somehow.

Tears spilled over to her cheeks. 'This is my friend's pet, Dominic. She loves it.' She clutched his arms. 'We have to find her. I know you think Minky is only a cat but Mel loves her. Really, truly, loves her. You can understand that, can't you? I know you don't want to get married or anything, but you understand love, right?'

Sure he did. He nodded. And loving a cat, even Minky, made perfect sense when Bella hiccupped through a sob and stared at him like that. 'We'll find her,' he promised, though he had no idea how he'd make good on it.

Fresh tears spilled down Bella's cheeks. A wave of protectiveness all but barrelled him over. With a muttered oath, he pulled her against his chest. He moved his hands up and down her back, trying to comfort her, hoping it would ease her distress. 'Don't cry,' he pleaded. 'We'll find Minky.' He eased back, his hands firm but gentle on her shoulders. 'You won't be able to see properly if you cry.'

'O-okay,' she hiccupped.

She took the handkerchief he held out, dried her eyes and then sent him a watery smile that ripped his heart clean out of his chest and threw it on the pavement at his feet. He sucked in a breath and tried to keep his footing. His insides shrivelled at the trust in her big brown eyes.

He had to swallow before he could speak. 'How about we search the rest of the alley first?'

She nodded. 'Okay.'

'You start on those boxes down there while I check the bins.'

She moved towards the other end of the alley. Dominic rested his hands on his knees for a moment. If Minky had been hit by a car the most likely place to dump the body would be the bin. He didn't want Bella finding the body.

His mobile rang. Damn, it'd be Marco again. Half-resigned, and with one eye firmly on Bella, he lifted the phone to his ear. 'Marco?' With a grimace, he held the phone away as Marco ranted at him in Italian. If he weren't so worried he'd have grinned at the similarities he could draw between father and daughter. He snapped to attention when he caught the word 'cat'.

'What did you say?' he demanded, breaking over Marco's ranting.

'I said you're not allowed pets in the apartments,' Marco hollered. 'Why didn't you check? The apartment manager rang and raked me—*me*—over the coals!'

'The cat's safe, then?'

'Yes, yes.'

Dominic started to laugh. Relief flooded him.

'This is no laughing—'

'Bella, we've found her!'

Bella raced to his side and gripped his arm, her eyes eager and hopeful. The air punched out of his body. She shook his arm. 'Dominic?'

He held the phone out to her. 'Your father.'

She frowned, took the phone. 'Papa?'

She promptly held the phone away from her ear. He could hear Marco's ranting from where he stood. He watched her listen carefully all the same. She grimaced apologetically to him. He couldn't help but grin at her.

Suddenly she grinned back. She covered the mouthpiece. 'Today,' she confided, 'he can yell at me all he wants.' Eventually she managed to end the call. She beamed up at him. 'Minky is in the apartment manager's office.'

Right. He took her arm to guide her out of the alley.

'Oh.' She stopped. 'One moment.'

She raced back to the homeless man. Dominic didn't hear what she said, but he saw her hand the man a card. 'What was that all about?' he asked.

'Oh, I'll tell you later.' She took his arm and herded him out of the alley. 'Hurry, we need to get our skates on. Papa is on his way and I need to get a cake on asap if we're not to have him grousing at us the entire night.'

Dominic laughed out loud at the expression that spread across Marco's face when he steamrolled into the apartment less than an hour later. And at the way he came to a dead halt and circled on the spot just like Bella had done the first time she'd stepped into the apartment. 'Pah!' His nose wrinkled. 'What is this place?'

'You tell us,' Bella said, kissing her father on the cheek. 'You organised it.'

Marco's face darkened as he swung to Dominic. 'Have you done anything to upset Katie, my PA?'

Dominic stiffened. 'No.'

Marco's eyes narrowed. 'Then what about her assistant, Gabby?'

He drew himself up. 'Certainly not.'

'There seems to have been some mix-up,' Bella cut in. 'Only one apartment was available. I doubt either Katie or Gabby were at fault.'

Marco turned to Bella. 'You have been baking, my girl?'

'I made you a sultana cake. And the coffee is brewing.'

He waggled a finger at her. 'You will not get around me so easily. Is this the offending cat?' He bent to glare into Minky's cage. Minky hissed. 'Pah!' Marco straightened. 'You must—'

He broke off to turn on the spot, his face a mixture of incredulity and disgust. 'How can you work here? There are no desks for you to spread out your files, your papers.'

'That has proved challenging,' Dominic allowed, accepting a coffee from the tray Bella brought out from the kitchen, along with a piece of still-warm cake. His mouth watered as a faint scent of lemon drifted up to him.

'You.' Marco rounded on Bella. 'Why did you not complain to me?'

Her tray shook. 'This is a business arrangement. Dominic and I have been making do. Now, drink your coffee, Papa, and have a piece of cake. I promise it is very good.'

It hit Dominic then how ill at ease Bella was with her father. Why? She all but glowed with love whenever she spoke of him.

He noticed then the unusual way Marco's glaze slid away from Bella's. What on earth? This pair adored each other! There was no reason for all this nonsensical awkwardness.

Marco took a sip of coffee. He took a bite of cake. Bella ignored her mug and plate. 'This is very good,' he grumbled. He took another bite and then slammed his plate to the table. 'But it does not change the fact that you must get rid of that cat!'

Bella raced across to pick up Minky's cage and clutch it to her chest. 'I can't!' For a moment Dominic thought she might cry. 'This is my friend Mel's cat. You remember Mel, Papa?'

'Yes, but—'

'Mel's father recently died.'

Dominic's cake—and Bella had been right, it was seriously good—halted halfway to his mouth. He lowered it back to his place. The stiffness shot out of Marco.

'Mel…' Bella hiccupped, but she didn't cry. 'Mel,' she started again, 'has gone to Melbourne to help her mother out for a bit and she couldn't take Minky as her mother is allergic to cats.'

Bella rested her cheek against the cage. To Dominic's astonishment, Minky pressed her face to Bella's and started to purr. 'Mel loves Minky. She told me it would break her heart if she had to put her into a cattery.' Bella lifted her head. 'Her heart, it needed a rest. She didn't need any more worries. She was so happy when I said I'd take care of Minky.'

Her friend had lost her father at about the same time Bella had found out how much she'd disappointed her own? An ache started up behind Dominic's eyes. She had a big heart, this woman, and she was doing what she could to make things right for everyone.

Marco swallowed once, twice. He cleared his throat. He pointed at Bella. 'You keep that cat!' He glared around the apartment. 'We will lose the apartment instead. I will organise for you both to be moved tomorrow. To a better, more suitable apartment where you can work properly and that will let you keep pets.'

'Thank you, Papa.'

Bella lowered the cage, but she didn't race across and engulf her father in a hug like he sensed she would like to. Marco didn't stride across and kiss Bella's cheek, as Dominic swore the older man ached to. He glanced from one to the other. Right.

He clapped his hands. 'The two of you, come with me.'

Bella blinked. 'But we haven't finished.'

'No arguments!'

She rolled her eyes at Marco. 'You see what I have to put up with?'

'I know, I know,' Marco muttered back. 'You see the way he speaks to me?'

Dominic hustled them out of the apartment. He took them down to the beach. Without a word he dropped to his knees in the sand and started digging.

Bella stared. Her eyes widened and then she started to laugh.

'What is this?' Marco demanded.

'We're building sandcastles,' Bella explained. 'Dominic has become quite the dab hand at them.' Her eyes danced. 'A champion, perhaps.'

Marco's jaw dropped. And then he shrugged out of his jacket and crouched down, his jaw thrust out. 'We'll see who the champion is, my girl.'

Bella knelt in the sand, too. They set about building turrets and moats and intricate canal systems. They set about building a world of dreams.

CHAPTER TEN

AT THE knock on his office door, Dominic glanced up and warmth surged through him. Bella stood in the doorway. His gut tightened at her smile, at the way she leaned a shoulder against the doorframe.

He gestured to a chair, but she shook her head. 'This is a flying visit, I'm afraid. I just wanted to thank you for yesterday.'

His blood throbbed. He leaned back and wished to heaven he'd never kissed this woman, because now that he had he wanted to taste her again and again.

He couldn't, of course. A taste wouldn't stop at one kiss and there was a whole host of reasons why he should avoid her.

'Not just for helping me look for Minky in the afternoon, but for smoothing the way between Papa and me.'

Yesterday—after they'd built a sandcastle that could only be described as a work of art—they'd gone back to the apartment where Bella had cooked the most divine pasta Dominic had ever tasted. They'd laughed and talked. All the tension and restraint had evaporated. Marco had regaled them with tales of the days he'd spent in Newcastle. It had been a good night.

He remembered Bella and Marco's laughter and shook his head. It had been a *great* night.

She twisted her hands together, shifted her weight from one leg to the other, met his gaze and then glanced away. He understood her tension; it spiralled through him too whenever they were alone.

'Bella, your father adores you.'

'Yes, I know.' She bit her lip as her gaze speared to his. 'So you have to see how important it is that, this time, I don't let him down.'

'You won't,' he assured her. Then he frowned. 'I understand you want to make your father proud, but it's more important that you are proud of yourself, you know, Bella.'

She blinked.

'Those two things aren't mutually exclusive.' He could see she didn't believe him. Somehow her very self-esteem was wrapped up in the success of her restaurant. It made him uneasy.

'I will be proud of myself once I've created the most fabulous restaurant my father has ever seen.'

'Speaking of which…' Her gaze slid away again and she worried at her thumbnail.

'Dominic—'

She started at the same time as he said, 'Bella.'

He gestured for her to continue, but she shook her head quickly. 'No, no, after you.'

He'd wanted to bring this up last night, but had been loath to raise it in front of Marco. 'Yesterday in the alley, you gave that homeless man a business card. Was it your business card?'

He knew she had a big heart, but if she wasn't careful someone could take serious advantage of her. He'd do whatever was necessary to prevent that.

She blinked, snapped upright, and for a moment he'd thought he'd offended her, then she laughed. 'What? Do you think I'm a complete moron?'

'Of course not.'

'You and Marco both think of me as a child, don't you?'

The memory of their kiss smacked into him. A child? Nope; absolutely not. That had to be the biggest, most wholehearted *'no'* in the history of man as far as he was concerned. He raised an eyebrow. Her cheeks flushed a deep pink. He shifted on his

chair and ordered himself to forget about that kiss. 'So, uh…'
He cleared his throat. 'Whose business card did you give him?'

She stared at him and then glanced down at her watch and
gave a tiny grimace. 'Ack, the time! I'll tell you about it later.'

'Bella!' He wasn't going to let her avoid him on this issue
for a second time. If anything happened to her, Marco would
hold him personally responsible.

He'd hold himself personally responsible. If anything happened to her, he'd never forgive himself.

She swung back. Challenge lit her eyes and she stuck out a
hip. 'Are you busy for the next hour or so?'

'Nothing that can't wait.'

'Well, if you want to find out what I'm up to, then walk
this way.'

She turned and sauntered away and didn't glance back to
see if he followed. He didn't hesitate. He rose to his feet and
set after her. One thing was certain—things were never bor-
ing when Bella was around. She had a talent for living that
he found addictive, a talent he still hadn't got to the heart of.

They stopped via the kitchen to collect two covered ham-
pers. He could tell at a glance how well respected she was by
the kitchen staff, how much they liked her. He insisted on carrying the larger hamper. He'd have carried the smaller one too
if she'd have let him.

'Where are we going?' he asked as she led him outside.

'You'll see.'

The sky was blue, the sun was shining, the faintest hint of
salt scented the air and suddenly he didn't want to press her.
He walked beside her, savoured the warmth of the sun on his
face instead and let her lead the way. He didn't doubt that it'd
all become clear soon enough.

They travelled down the pedestrian mall into the city centre and, although Bella's steps were brisk with purpose, he
found the muscles in his neck started to loosen. He hadn't even
known they were tight.

'Look.' She pointed. 'Don't you just love those plane trees?'

A line of them marched down the paved path of the mall; their leaves, a young green, had just started to unfurl. She tossed her head. 'I'm going to come back here in summer. I want to swim at the beach and see these plane trees in all their glory and—'

'Eat ice-cream and build sandcastles,' he finished for her.

'Ooh, yes! It sounds divine, doesn't it?'

It did. He could afford to holiday anywhere in the world, but Bella was right—Newcastle in summer sounded divine.

'Up this way.' She pointed and led him up a side street. 'And here we are.' She ducked inside a brick building that was non-descript and a bit shabby. Dominic read the plaque by the door and his jaw dropped. What on earth? He shot inside after her but she'd already disappeared from view.

The interior was dim and a little musty. He had to wait for his eyes to adjust before following the sound of voices out towards the back of the building.

He pulled up short in a wide doorway. Approximately twenty men, most of them getting on in years, and all of them as shabby as the building itself, sat in a large dining room. Something clenched up hard and tight inside him as he glanced around.

Hell! He swore under his breath. *Double hell!* Why had Bella brought him to this place? Why did she want to show him these men?

Men who reminded him so vividly of his father.

As if his thoughts had conjured her, Bella waltzed into the room from a doorway at the side and a cheer went up. She carried three trays laden with tiny vol-au-vent pastries. She set a tray on each of the three tables. Then she stood back, hands on hips, as their contents were promptly devoured. He couldn't believe what short work the men made of them.

'Well?' she demanded. 'Are they better than yesterday's or not?'

A great din erupted. Bella shushed the men and then demanded a show of hands.

This was how Bella was spending her lunch breaks—at St Xavier's Men's Shelter? He caught sight of a battered and patched coat and the memories hit him: coming home from school to find his father passed out; the smell of cheap port; the utter poverty and the dirtiness of it all. He backed up a step. He'd left that world behind. He had no intention of revisiting it.

But more memories bombarded him, and along with them the same old sense of helplessness and powerlessness he'd experienced as a child. The fear and failure that had gripped him as he'd slowly faced the fact that he couldn't help his father, that he couldn't stop him drinking. The overwhelming sense of inadequacy. And the fear that he would end up the same way.

None of it had been his fault. He knew that now, but…

His chest hollowed out. His eyes burned. Why hadn't he been enough for his father? If Dominic ever had a son, he would never emotionally desert him. He'd look after him. Love him.

He swung away and moved back through the building, needing to feel the warmth of the sun on his face and draw cleansing breaths into his lungs. A hand on his arm pulled him to a stop. 'Dominic, where are you going?'

He rounded on her. 'Away from this place! Why the hell did you bring me here?'

'Because…' Comprehension dawned in the soft depths of her eyes. 'Oh! Your father.' Her hand flew to her mouth. 'Dominic, I'm sorry. I didn't think of that.' She pulled her hand away. 'The business card I gave the man in the alley, it was for this place.'

Of course it was.

'Dominic—'

'No!' He didn't know what she meant to ask him, but the answer was no. 'I've left that world behind.'

These men would be running away from something, letting

someone down. He refused to be party to that. They didn't deserve Bella's food, her smiles or her charity. And they didn't deserve his!

'Right. Fine.' She swallowed and gestured. 'May I have my basket before you leave, please?'

That was when he realised he still clenched the handle of the hamper in his right hand. A hamper that no doubt contained the men's dinner. He shoved it at her.

She took it gingerly. 'Thank you.'

He couldn't help noticing that she held it in both hands and he frowned. It was pretty heavy.

Not his problem!

But before he could spin away she spoke again. 'You have left that world behind, Dominic, well and truly. You are a different man than your father. You will never suffer the same fate. I wonder why you can't believe that.'

He did believe that. He would never go back to that life. *Never.*

'Life broke your father's heart and I know that's why you protect yours so fiercely.'

He blinked.

'But can't you open it just a crack, be grateful for everything you do have, and give back just a little bit?'

He gaped at her. 'Grateful?'

'Yes, grateful!' she snapped. 'Grateful that you have an intelligent brain in your head and that you had the opportunity to go to university and build a good life for yourself. Grateful that you work for one of the most fantastic companies on the planet. Grateful that you have nice things—clothes, a ritzy car and no doubt a nice apartment.

'Damn it, Dominic! You should be grateful that illness or injury or events haven't conspired to prevent you from achieving all that you have. And now you want to bellyache about giving a little to those who haven't been as lucky as you? Pah!'

If she hadn't been holding the basket, he knew she'd have flung a hand in the air to indicate her disgust.

'But before you can do that you'd have to forgive your father, and you don't want to, do you?'

Every word sliced through him.

'Perhaps you ought to think about it, because as far as I can see the only person you're hurting is yourself.'

He couldn't think of a single retort. Without another word, she turned and headed back towards the dining room.

Bella's heart gave a thump that almost knocked the breath from her body when she glanced up five minutes later to find Dominic silhouetted in the kitchen doorway. Her complete happiness at seeing him took her off-guard.

She swallowed. That couldn't be good.

But the fact he'd stayed made her want to seize his hands and dance him around the room.

Only, he didn't look as if he wanted to be danced around the room. He looked as if he wanted to throttle her. She might've shamed him into staying, but that didn't mean she'd reconciled him to this place or these people.

Her mouth went dry. It had been a mistake to bring him here.

'What can I do?' His voice was clipped and short.

She wanted to tell him to go, but didn't know how to do so without making the situation worse. 'Potatoes,' she finally said. 'We have a lot of potatoes to peel.'

Without another word, he moved to the mountain of potatoes on the opposite bench and set to work.

'*Signorina* Bella, have you spoken to Mr Dominic yet about the budget?'

Bella pulled her mind back from pictures of Dominic helping to serve lunch at St Xavier's earlier in the day. From pictures of broad, drool-worthy shoulders tight with tension and a beautiful mouth set in a hard straight line.

He'd frozen her out. He hadn't spoken to her. He'd barely glanced at her.

'Uh, no.' She and Luigi had spent the afternoon putting a couple of sous chefs through their paces and were now going through the paperwork. Though in truth Bella had been leaving most of that to Luigi. She didn't have a talent for paperwork.

Luigi turned reproachful eyes to her. 'But you promised, *signorina*. That's why you went to see Mr Dominic this morning.'

She knew why Luigi was so worried. They would have to start hiring new chefs soon, but Luigi refused to do that until he had the official nod from Dominic. They couldn't leave it much longer.

'We got side-tracked.' She didn't know what on earth had prompted her to invite Dominic along to the men's shelter, but since his less-than-enthusiastic reaction she'd been kicking herself for the impulse. She hadn't meant to rake up painful memories for him. And, to make matters worse, had it really been necessary to abuse him like she had? *Nice one, Bella.*

After they'd cleaned up the lunch at St Xavier's, they'd walked back to the hotel in silence. Dominic's brooding frown had prohibited conversation. Bringing up questions about budgets hadn't seemed wise.

It didn't seem wise now, either. She'd stirred terrible memories for Dominic, wounding memories, without warning and without giving him a chance to compose himself. The last thing he'd want right now was to see her. She knew that deep in her bones. The problem was, she'd already delayed this budget issue for too long. She hadn't meant to, but...

She pushed her shoulders back, pulled in a breath and consoled herself with the thought that, once she did have Dominic's official go-ahead, her restaurant would be the best restaurant Newcastle had ever seen. Marco would love it. And he'd be proud of her.

She rubbed her hands in anticipation of that. She could see

the glory of their opening night: her father and Dominic in tuxedos; she in something black and sophisticated; their dining room filled with beautiful, glittering people and her father enjoying the company; the plaudits; savouring the food. And then her father looking over at her with pride in his eyes, acknowledging she had created the restaurant of his dreams. Her heart started to expand in her chest.

'Bella!'

A rap on the door snapped her to. Dominic. Her blood heated up and all the fine hairs on her arms and the nape of her neck lifted to attention.

'A word, if I may?'

He didn't smile. She swallowed. 'Of course.'

'In my office.'

He turned and left. She swung around at Luigi's groan. 'What?'

He shook his head. 'I do not think you should keep Mr Dominic waiting, *Signorina* Bella.'

She recalled the stern line of Dominic's mouth and with a nod she set off after him. Did he mean to have a go at her about St Xavier's? She worried at her bottom lip. She put in long hours at the hotel. She was entitled to a lunch break. What she chose to do on said lunch break was her own concern, right?

She all but skidded into Dominic's office. 'Look, before you say anything,' she started, 'I want you to know that the hotel is not funding those St Xavier lunches. I've merely offered my services to help out for two lunches a week, that's all. And I'm not using the hotel's resources.' She grimaced. 'Well, except for those little pastries I took in.' She lifted her chin. 'But that was legitimate market research.' And she hadn't been able to resist taking the men in a little treat. They had so little to look forward to.

He pursed his lips. 'I haven't asked you in here to talk about the men's shelter. If you think it's a charity we should be supporting, I'd urge you to put a proposal together and submit it to me. We have a charity budget for such things.'

But even as he said the words his shoulders, his back and his jaw all tensed up. She moistened suddenly dry lips. His body language told her he would *never* support the men's shelter. She had an awful foreboding that he may never forgive her for what she'd put him through today. 'Dominic, I want to apologise for earlier and—'

A hand slashing through the air cut her off. 'This is what I want to talk to you about.'

He thrust a sheet of paper at her. She took it and then swallowed. 'Oh, my revised budget.'

He folded his arms and raised an eyebrow. He didn't sit. He didn't invite her to sit. 'I've been meaning to talk to you about it for a while now.'

'And why haven't you?'

She hated his hard, unrelenting tone. She wished they could be having this conversation on any day other than today. Or, if it had to be today, that they'd had it this morning before they'd set off for St Xavier's.

She swallowed. 'Well, I started to bring it up that afternoon Minky went missing, but then everything else went out of my head except for finding her. Then Papa was there and it didn't seem right to talk shop. One of the reasons I dropped by this morning was to talk about it, but we got side-tracked.'

'There have been abundant opportunities for you to approach me about this.'

It was true she was making excuses. 'That stupid kiss!' she suddenly burst out. 'It made things awkward. And all of a sudden you were never at the apartment.'

'I have always been available during working hours here in my office!'

That was true, too. She eyed him uneasily. 'You can be a nice man sometimes, Dominic, but you can also be a scary boss.'

His jaw dropped.

'Though I can see now how foolish it has been to put off talking to you about this new budget.'

'That's not a budget. It's a fantasy!'

Each and every one of her muscles locked. He couldn't mean that. He was just angry with her because of the men's shelter. Once he cooled down…

He snatched the budget from her hand and slammed it to his desk. He pointed. 'What is this particular costing for?'

She peered to where his finger stabbed the neat whiteness of the printed page. 'That's for new tables for the dining room. That interior decorator knew nothing! We need glass table-tops that will take advantage of the ocean setting and reflect it back into the room. The light in the evenings is amazing, spectacular, and—'

'No.'

She drew back. 'I beg your pardon?'

'I said, no. You are not getting new tables, Bella.'

'But—'

'You can argue till you're blue in the face, but I will not budge on this.'

He pulled a pen from his pocket and drew a line through the item.

'What about this costing? It says chefs. All the staff have already been employed.'

'Ah…' He couldn't argue with this. 'I want to institute French service, you see.'

He stared at her blankly.

'It means that many of the dishes are finished off by chefs at the tables. It turns the preparation of the food into an event!' She made a wide gesture with her arms in an attempt to il-lustrate the drama. 'Our patrons will love it, but we'd need to hire additional chefs.'

She had a sudden brainwave. 'Now, because we need ad-ditional room for the chefs and their mobile cooking stations, there will actually be fewer tables in the dining room, so the new tables you've scrawled from the budget would—'

'Fewer tables?' he barked. 'We'd be serving fewer patrons each night? How is that good business practice?' he demanded.

'Well, because there's so much preparation and show involved, that would be reflected in the menu prices.'

'Fewer people paying more money?'

Her mouth went dry at his expression. All she could manage was a weak, 'Uh-huh.'

He snatched up the budget. 'Follow me.'

'Where?' She scampered after him.

'To the kitchen. I want Luigi's input on this.'

'This is all my doing, not Luigi's.' She didn't want to get Luigi into trouble.

'That's more than obvious.' He stopped dead to glare at her. 'He has a better business head on his shoulders than you ever will.' He set off again. 'It is he who should've been given the restaurant-manager position, not you.'

The breath punched out of her body. He couldn't mean that! She tried to swallow her panic as she raced after him again. She had to save her restaurant from his hard, iceman heart.

'Luigi?' Dominic pushed into the kitchen. Bella was right at his heels. 'Have all the staff left for the day?'

Luigi glanced up from his station at the computer. 'Yes, sir.'

'Then it's just Bella, you and me here?'

Luigi rose. 'That's right, Mr Dominic.'

'Good. I have just been going over this revised budget of Bella's and it is unworkable.'

'It is not!'

Dominic ignored her. 'She tells me she wants to use French service in the restaurant.'

'Yes, sir. It is very spectacular. The patrons would enjoy it.'

'But it means higher staffing and equipment costs and we would be serving fewer customers, is that right?'

Luigi threw Bella an agonised glance. 'Uh, yes, sir.'

Dominic lifted the budget. 'That is unacceptable.'

Bella gripped her hands together. Her heart hammered in her chest. 'The French service is *vital* to our restaurant's success.'

Dominic stared at her, his gaze lowering to her lips, before he snapped away and swung back to Luigi. 'Is that true? If I veto this French service of Bella's, is the restaurant doomed?'

Luigi shuffled his feet and tossed her another agonised glance.

'Stop bullying him, Dominic.'

'I am not bullying anyone. I am asking for answers!'

He had a heart of ice! And he was determined to punish her—for taking him to the men's shelter; for growing up in the lap of luxury and not appreciating it as she should've done; for not making the most of the opportunities she'd been given.

Perhaps she deserved to be punished. *It is he who should've been given the restaurant-manager position, not you.*

Stupid. Failure. Fool.

No! She clenched her hands. She wanted—needed—to create the best restaurant she could. For Papa. She dragged in a breath and tried to rein in her panic. 'I already know what Luigi will say. He'd say we could use American service instead and all will be well. Not spectacular, but well.'

'And what's wrong with that?'

Couldn't he see? 'It's what every other restaurant in town uses. We need to stand out and—'

'That's what was budgeted for previously?'

'Yes, but—'

'Blue in the face,' he growled. 'Won't budge.'

He got his pen out again and scrawled a line through the budget for new staff and new equipment. Her hands shook. He was ruining her restaurant!

He flicked the page. 'And what's this?'

She stared to where he pointed. She had to blink a couple of times to clear her vision. 'That's the fee for the entertainment in the restaurant on opening night. She's a famous soul singer.'

The pulse in Dominic's jaw twitched. He stared at her in disbelief. 'And she costs this much?'

She pushed her hands behind her back to hide the way they shook. 'She'll be a real draw-card.' The pulse in her throat beat so frantically she found it hard to speak and although it felt impossible she managed a smile. 'She's also Marco's favourite singer.'

'She won't be if he ever saw this bill! Luigi, give me an alternative.'

No! She stared wildly from one man to the other. This couldn't be happening. Her lungs constricted until she could barely breathe. Her vision of their brilliant opening night fractured, cracked and dissolved.

Luigi glanced from one to the other. He shook his head and sighed. 'They are not in the same league, you understand, but there is a local jazz trio who are very good.'

'Hire them,' Dominic ordered, slashing a line through that item too with his pen of death. Bella wanted to snatch it from his hand and draw a line through him!

'What is this?'

Thankfully this time he addressed Luigi because Bella wasn't sure she had the capacity to speak.

'It's new artwork for the restaurant.'

'We already have artwork.' His pen went to work again.

Bella found her voice. 'Do you need Luigi any more this afternoon, Dominic?'

'No, I think we're done.'

She turned to Luigi. 'I know you have a parent and teachers' evening up at Rilla's school tonight, Luigi. I also know you were in early this morning, so if you wanted to head off that is okay.'

The words were barely out of her mouth when Luigi snatched up his coat and started to back out the door. 'Good afternoon, *Signorina* Bella, Mr Dominic.'

'Good afternoon, Luigi,' she called after him. Dominic merely nodded.

'Bella, I'm sorry, but—'

'This is all to punish me for taking you to St Xavier's today, isn't it? For bringing back bad memories for you.' She could do nothing to disguise the way her voice shook.

His brow darkened. 'This has nothing to do with that. *Nothing!*' He slashed a hand through the air. 'This is purely business.'

'I don't believe you.' Her mouth went drier than a desert as the truth hit her. 'You've had a bee in your bonnet about me from the day we started. You're angry that I got all the advantages in life when you had none. You're angry that I've wasted those advantages. And now, *now* you want me to fail!' He'd warned her he didn't want her on his team. He'd told her he'd had no faith in her. And yet she'd thought...

Her eyes burned. Her head throbbed. 'You've been waiting for a moment like this so you could sabotage me.'

His head reared back. His mouth became a thin white line. 'I'm going to overlook that comment because I know how disappointed you are.'

'Disappointed?' That didn't begin to describe it. He wanted to wreck everything she'd been working so hard towards. Everything!

His eyes flashed as he tore the budget up into tiny pieces and threw them in the air. 'You will work within the budget you were given, Bella. End of story.'

She stared at the tiny pieces of paper fluttering on the air about her. 'That took me hours,' she whispered.

'Hours poorly spent,' he snapped.

She had to swallow back a wave of nausea that rolled through her then. She could suddenly see the opening night in the restaurant and her father's barely disguised disappointment and resignation. His face would shutter closed. He'd turn away.

She couldn't stand it!

Dominic fished a key from his pocket and held it out to her. 'Our new apartment is ready and waiting.' He named the apartment complex. It was only a block away. 'Marco organised for all of our things to be moved there earlier today. I suggest you head there now to compose yourself. You won't get any good work done when you're like this.'

She took the key.

Dominic had won.

She turned and fled.

CHAPTER ELEVEN

DOMINIC threw his pen down with a less than subtle curse and gave up trying to work.

Iceman, he reminded himself. That was what his business associates called him. He wasn't feeling too ice-cold at the moment, though. In fact, he never felt like an iceman when Bella was around.

Those big wounded eyes of hers rose in his mind. Again. He pressed a thumb and forefinger to his eyes and rubbed them. He'd been hard on her. Had he really torn her budget up into tiny pieces? Had he really told her that Luigi was a better choice for the job than her?

With a groan he dropped his head to his hands and scratched them both back through his hair. That wasn't true. Luigi might have more experience and a better business brain, but Bella had vision and passion to spare. She just needed to channel it in the right directions.

'So what did you say it for you tactless idiot?' he muttered under his breath. He'd never lost it like that with an employee before. Never.

Why had he done so today? Because she'd called him a scary boss?

He rolled his shoulders. He hadn't liked hearing that. In fact, he'd hated it. He'd always prided himself on his approachability. For the first time he'd seen that maybe his pride had been misplaced. Icemen weren't known for their warmth and empathy. Maybe it wasn't just his business rivals who saw him as ruthless and cold.

But he'd been called far worse things than a scary boss and he hadn't lost it.

She'd mentioned that darn kiss!

He leapt up, strode to the window and stared out at the beach. He shoved his hands into his pockets. He couldn't do anything about that kiss. He couldn't take it back. He couldn't repeat it. Yet every cell in his body clamoured to whenever she was near.

He rolled his shoulders again and tried to loosen the knots in them. All that tension, it might've made him a tad testy.

She'd gone white when he'd told her Luigi should've been given the job.

He swiped a hand through the air and gave up lying to himself. It wasn't the 'scary boss' comment. It wasn't the kiss. It was that darn men's shelter! It had taken him back to a dark place, a place where he'd been hungry and cold and powerless to do anything about it. That sense of helplessness had eaten at his soul all afternoon.

It had felt good to vent at Bella, to yell at her, to throw his weight around and veto all of her ideas. And to feel righteous while doing it. The realisation made him feel sick. He hadn't been wrong about the budget—Bella had lost her head and gone over the top with that—but the way he'd approached their discussion...

He'd managed to remind himself of his power, to reinforce his autonomy and authority, but he'd made it personal. He'd been completely unprofessional.

Why? Because, where his father was concerned, Bella had been right—he had been holding a grudge in his heart for too long.

He pressed the heel of his hand to his brow. All she'd been trying to do was create the restaurant of Marco's dreams, and he'd shot her ideas down in flames. Just like that. He should've handled it with more compassion and tact. Shown her some understanding and explained why he'd had to make the decision he had.

He should've been around for her a whole lot more these last three weeks—offering her support, advice. For heaven's sake, Marco had told him she knew next to nothing about management and business. He'd left her to flounder, knowing of her inexperience.

You've been waiting for a moment like this so you could sabotage me!

Garbage.

Was it? a little voice whispered through him. He'd resented her from the first—the pampered only daughter, the spoiled little rich girl. Only Bella wasn't spoiled. She worked hard. She had a big heart, and he...

His hands clenched. Acid burned his tongue. Mean-spirited and cowardly, that was how he'd acted. He hadn't been any kind of coach or mentor to her. She stirred emotions in him he didn't want stirred. She'd challenged him about his past and his current attitude, and he'd found it hard to deal with. His solution had been to avoid her.

To then jump on her like he had, when she'd made a mistake, that was patently unfair. He had to take a portion of the blame for her ridiculous budget.

He was a classic example of how not to do things!

He paced up and down in front of the window.

This is all to punish me!

So much of her self-respect was invested in that restaurant. He'd torn her vision to shreds, shot down her dream.

There had been something in her face. Shock, for sure, but something else, too. Defeat?

Despair!

Dominic stiffened. 'Oh, hell!' He grabbed his jacket off the back of his chair and bolted for the door.

* * *

Dominic burst into their new apartment, saw Bella's suitcases packed and lined up beside the sofa and swore under his breath. Why the hell had he been so heavy handed with her?

Bella appeared in the doorway, towing her last suitcase. Her jaw slackened when she saw him. 'What are you doing here?'

Damn it! She really had intended to do a runner without telling him first. He fought back the anger that clogged his throat, the disappointment, tossed his keys onto the small foyer-table and moved more fully into the room. 'I decided to take the rest of the day off, too. I was curious to see the apartment.'

He made himself glance around. 'Marco has surpassed himself this time. This is a marked improvement.'

The living room, dining room and kitchen were all open-plan, the kitchen divided from the rest of the room by a long, chest-high bench. The apartment was decorated in varying shades of blues and greys. Light poured in at wide windows that stretched along two entire walls. Bella shifted from one foot to the other and then pointed. 'There's the most fabulous view of the harbour.'

'You'll be able to watch the container ships come in to your heart's content,' he said, bending down to release Minky from her cage. She rubbed against his legs before running off to explore.

'What are you doing?' Bella gaped at him. 'Do you know how long it took me to—?'

She broke off. He straightened. 'I'm letting her out to stretch her legs and to explore her new home. She must be tired of being cooped up.' There was not a chance Bella would leave without Minky.

He grabbed two of her suitcases. 'You'd think the moving guys would've had the decency to put your bags in your room.' He strove for a light tone. 'Though they probably couldn't believe that all these bags belonged to just one person.'

'What do you think you're doing?' She seized the bags and pulled them from his grasp.

He'd hoped she'd have the sense to play along with his charade. 'Helping you get settled.'

'But I—'

'And then I wanted to apologise to you.'

She tossed her head. 'For ruining my entire life?'

He had to smile at her exaggeration. 'For handling that budget issue so badly. I was unduly hard on you and that wasn't fair. I'm sorry.'

She eyed him for a moment. 'Does that mean you're going to increase my budget?'

'No, I'm not.'

'Pah!' She threw a hand in the air. 'Forget it, Dominic. I'm leaving.'

'No, you're not.'

She thrust her chin out. 'Do you mean to stop me?'

'Yes. Physically, if necessary.' He kept his tone even. He prayed she wouldn't test him on this. 'You gave your father your word that you would see this project through. I mean to see that you do.'

'When you tie my hands?' She flung both arms out and started to pace. 'How is it possible?' She rounded on him. 'You make it impossible!'

'All this simply because I rein in a few extravagances?'

'Rein in?' Her jaw dropped. 'You wreck my entire vision. You tell me that I'm not good enough for the job! You tell me I waste my time. At least I put all of me into a project—all my heart and soul. You don't even have a heart! But you're right, I have been wasting my time. You think Luigi is the right person for the job, then go ahead and give it to him!'

She seized two suitcases, but before she could walk off with them he seized her wrists. She immediately dropped them. Beneath his hands her skin was warm and her pulse pounded. He let go of her again quick smart. 'That was a stupid thing for me to say. I didn't mean it. I lost my temper. I've been off-kilter even since I stepped foot inside that men's shelter. It's the only excuse I can offer, and I am sincerely sorry.'

Her mouth dropped open. The need to kiss her grew so great he had to clench his hands to stop from reaching for her. 'I blame myself for the mistakes you made with that stupid budget.'

She blinked. She folded her arms. 'Stupid?' Her voice wobbled.

'And I blame myself for losing my cool like I did and for not explaining things properly to you, but let's get one thing clear, I am not going to blame myself for your lack of perseverance now, for your lack of a backbone.'

'My...?'

'It's about time you grew up. If you make a promise to someone, you don't turn your back on it and them and run away the moment things get tough. You've let your father down in the past, but you promised him those days were over. Well, prove it!'

She'd gone white.

'Yes, you're passionate. But you take things to heart too easily. You fly off the handle too quickly. You have a brain in that beautiful head of yours. Use it!'

He didn't know what he'd just said, but Bella turned paler than white. He pulled in a breath and eyed her for a moment. She didn't move. She didn't even blink. 'I, uh... Bella, I think you should sit down.'

He tried to take her arm, alarm surging through him, but she pulled out of his grip. With eyes that looked huge and bruised in such a colourless face, she edged away from him. She hardly seemed even to breathe. What the hell had he said?

'Bella, breathe!' he ordered, suddenly afraid that she'd pass out. When he made a move towards her, she turned and fled down the hallway. He followed but he wasn't quick enough. The bathroom door was slammed into place and the lock rammed home.

He stared. What the hell had he said?

He pressed an ear to the door but not a single sound emerged.

Bella curled into a ball on the bathroom floor, pressed her cheek to the cold of the tiles and did what she could to push the panic out of her lungs so she could breathe again. She squeezed her eyes tight and started to shake.

Dominic had so deftly stripped her of all her defences...

She pressed a fist to her mouth. When he'd said that she had a brain in her head, she hadn't known what else to do except retreat. She'd needed to hide from eyes that saw too much. She'd needed to hide from the hard anger in them, from the disappointment, and from the iceman coldness that would eventually chill them.

He was waiting for her outside the door; she knew he was. Him and all her fears.

You have a brain in your head.

Yes, she did, but it wasn't worth a tuppence. And when he found that out... When Papa found that out...

Her throat closed over. She clenched her eyes so tight stars burst behind them.

'Bella?' The door rattled.

Her throat was so thick she could barely swallow, let alone speak.

It's about time you grew up...

'Bella! So help me, I'll break this door down!'

He would, too. She opened her eyes. It was time to stop hiding. She paused and then hauled herself into a sitting position. It took all her effort but eventually she managed to swallow the lump in her throat. 'I'll be out in a moment.'

'You mean that?'

She wanted to answer with a scornful, 'of course'. Or a, 'guess you'll find out'. But she didn't have the energy for either. Or the heart. 'Yes.' That was all she could manage.

She heard him move away from the door. She pushed to her

feet and stared at her reflection in the mirror. Ugh; vampires and zombies had nothing on her. She splashed water onto her face and tried to pinch some colour into her cheeks, wondering how her face could be so colourless when it burned so hot. Or how it was possible for the rest of her to go so cold.

She rinsed all her make-up off and that made her feel even barer, but it couldn't be helped. No make-up was preferable to smudged make-up.

She stared at the door. She closed her eyes and pulled three deep breaths into her body. Only then did she open the door and walk back out into the living room. All her suitcases had been taken back to her room.

It's about time you grew up.

Dominic was right. It was time to face this like an adult. Who knew? He might even help her find a way to break this gently to Papa, to help her reconcile her father to his daughter's serious shortcomings.

Dominic's narrow-eyed gaze travelled over every inch of her. He finally gave a curt nod. 'You look better.'

'I'm sorry. I felt unwell for a moment. The bathroom seemed the best place to be.'

He gestured. 'I made coffee.'

Instant; she didn't have the energy to argue, or even to grimace. She took a cup and then a seat on the enormous L-shaped sofa. Dominic sat, too. He left two full seat-cushions between them as if afraid of crowding her. She noted, though, that he'd positioned himself between her and the door.

Minky jumped up beside her, meowed and then settled herself on the back of the sofa at Bella's neck, as if she sensed Bella needed comfort. Absurdly, it made her want to cry.

She dragged in a shaky breath, glanced at Dominic and then glanced away again. She didn't want to see his eyes turn hard and cynical as she said what she had to say.

She sipped her coffee, grimaced and set it down. 'Let's not drag this out longer than necessary, Dominic. The truth of the matter is you were right from the start—I'm actually not up to doing this job. I have no business qualifications, no real experience.' She swallowed. 'I'm not even a properly qualified chef.'

He stared at her for a moment and then he shrugged. 'The way you cook, Bella, speaks for itself.'

That, at least, was nice of him to say, but she shook her head. 'If I stay I will wreck Marco's restaurant. That…' She gulped and tried to force steel into her voice. 'That would be a hundred times worse than disappointing him by walking away now.'

Minky rubbed her head against Bella's nape. Bella had to swallow hard.

Dominic stared at her for a moment and then he leant towards her. 'You really believe this?'

It's about time you grew up.

'I know it. Mentally—intellectually—I'm not up to scratch. I'm not clever or smart.' She sagged back against the sofa. 'In fact, I'm stupid. I can't even do long division!'

She tried not to flinch at the way his jaw dropped, at the shock in his eyes. 'What the hell—? What's long division got to do with anything?'

'It's just one example of my lack of intelligence.' She lifted her chin. Her head had never felt heavier. 'It's time to stop lying to you. It's time to stop lying to Marco. And it's time I stopped lying to myself. I'm sure there are worse things in the world than not being very bright. I might not be smart, but I'm kind to animals and I can cook a truly divine chocolate mud cake. I have a lot of friends and I love my family. I have to stop wishing for more.'

Frown lines furrowed Dominic's brow. 'Let's get one thing straight right now—you don't need to know how to do long division.'

'But I do need to know how to do up a spreadsheet and a profit-and-loss statement and basic accounting and…and a budget! Most of the time all that stuff is double Dutch to me.'

'You did just fine on the budget.'

'You slammed it! You said it was a fantasy.'

'The fantasy was the amount of money you were asking for. The document itself was perfectly acceptable—correctly laid out and costed accurately.' He sat back. 'I don't doubt for a moment that the restaurant you could create with that much money would be spectacular, but Marco has been very specific about the amount of money he is prepared to pour into the Newcastle Maldini. If I don't stick to that, he told me I'd be out on my ear.'

'He did not!'

'He did.' One corner of his mouth hooked up. 'But he didn't mean it. Doesn't change the fact that I want to do a good job for him.'

It hadn't occurred to her that Dominic might be under as much pressure as she was. She resisted the allure of his smile, though.

She shook her head. 'I must've got lucky with that budget then, Dominic. You won't know this because Marco hushed it up, but I flunked my final exams at school. After Mama died… Well, I didn't study, and I didn't pay attention in class.' She hadn't done much of anything for eighteen months. 'That's not meant to excuse my lack of application at the time, it's just what happened. When I got it together again, I just seemed to be playing endless catch-up.'

The sudden warmth in his eyes threatened to wrap around her if she let it, to cocoon her. She refused to let it. It was a lie. 'Papa pulled strings to get me into university but—' she shrugged '—I couldn't keep up there either.'

'Why didn't Marco help you? Get you tutors?'

'Oh, I never told him! I was too ashamed.' He had been so disappointed in her school marks. She hadn't been able to face that again. 'And he'd already done so much.'

'So you left uni and bounced from one job to another.'

She stared at her hands. 'Nothing worked out. Either I couldn't do the work or it was so absolutely basic, I grew so bored I thought I would die.' And that disappointment she'd been trying save her father from, it had happened again anyway. 'Eventually I fled to Italy to help my aunt and uncle in their restaurant.' When they'd offered her the job she'd jumped at it. Not least because she'd thought removing herself from Marco's presence would save him from any further embarrassment.

'But you said you loved working in the restaurant, that it was great.'

'It was.' Just for a moment she allowed herself a smile. 'I learned so much and discovered a passion and talent for cooking that I never knew I had. It was a revelation.' Her relief, her gratitude at finding her place in the world, had been immense.

Her smile dissolved. 'But it made me cocky and arrogant, foolhardy.'

Dominic's eyes narrowed.

'I should've been content with being a cook, but no. Just because I could run my uncle's restaurant, I thought that meant I could create the perfect restaurant for Papa's hotel. I'd been looking for a reason to come home—I missed Papa—and the Newcastle Maldini provided the perfect excuse. I thought I could show him that I was all grown up and that I could be useful to him in the business, an asset.'

But she'd been wrong.

'The hotel is so much bigger. There's so much more to understand and keep on top of.' There were so many more ways to fail. 'It's not just the restaurant, but room service and function rooms. And there are so many spreadsheets!'

'All that long division?' Dominic murmured.

She swallowed and nodded. She'd known he'd understand.

'Bella, I can teach you long division.'

She glanced up.

'I can teach you everything you need to know about spreadsheets, basic accounting and budgets.'

He could? Hope she hadn't even known she'd nurtured lifted

through her. She tried to stamp it out. It was pointless hope. Dominic would try to teach her but her defective brain would refuse to grasp all it needed to.

'You may not be able to see it, but you are most definitely an asset to the hotel.'

'That's not true. What I have done, Luigi could've done quicker and with less fuss.'

'Luigi would still be buying sub-standard stock from his brother-in-law. Luigi would not have come up with the cooking-club idea or the social outings for the staff that you have. Luigi would not have made me see how important the personality of the hotel is to its success.

'Bella, you aren't stupid. You fell behind at school and the teachers you've had since—at university and in the work-place—haven't recognised your need. I'd suggest that's because you've been so clever at hiding it.'

She could feel herself flush.

'You are not stupid. You've lost your confidence, that's all.'

No, he was wrong. Oh, she'd lost her confidence all right, but it was because intellectually she wasn't up to much.

He must've seen that sentiment in her face. 'Fine,' he snapped. 'Let's play a game. You can't have your beautiful glass-topped tables in the restaurant. Tell me what you dislike about the current set-up.'

'No colour,' she responded instantly. 'Wooden tables with white-on-white tablecloths.' The entire room would lack personality.

'You can't have those new tables, but what else could you do to fix that lack of colour?'

She thought for a moment. 'Beige, sand-coloured tablecloths with light blue overlays.' That would look quite nice. She could manage a sophisticated beach theme with that.

'See? You just found a solution to one of your budget problems like that.' He snapped his fingers.

She had?

'You just defined a problem and came up with a solution—' he checked his watch '—in under a minute. That is not a sign of someone with a poor intellect.'

Really?

'You have a lot to offer. Your passion for this hotel has infused its every corner—even to me. You have made me better at my job with all your challenges. Now let me help you become better at yours.'

She stared at him. She could see he meant every word. Did she dare? To take him up on his offer meant risking failure.

'But I need you fully committed,' he warned. 'Once we start, you aren't backing out.'

But it meant the possibility of success, too. Minky batted her hair. 'You really think I can do it?'

'I'm certain of it.'

She bit her lip. She pulled in a breath. Finally, she thrust out her hand, choosing to trust him. 'You have yourself a deal.'

'Excellent!'

When he took her hand and smiled at her, she felt as if she'd won the lottery.

He didn't let go of her hand. 'You don't need to prove yourself to Marco, Bella. He is already proud of you, regardless of what you think.' His hand tightened. 'But I do think you need to prove it to yourself.'

She blinked. She pulled her hand from his because it was starting to feel far too comfortable there.

'We are going to make the hotel work, Bella. But there is something else I think you need to consider, and I want you to think about it long and hard.'

He sounded so suddenly serious that her mouth dried.

'Do you really want to work in your father's company? I know you want Marco to be proud of you, but you don't have to work in his company to do that. What is it *you* want to do?'

She opened her mouth. She closed it again. She'd been so focussed on not failing, on doing what she thought her father wanted, that it wasn't a question she'd actually asked herself. 'I don't know,' she confessed. 'All I know is that I don't want to keep bouncing from one job to the next.'

'What part of this job makes you happiest?'

'Working in the kitchen,' she answered without hesitation. 'Cooking, planning the menus, training the chefs.'

He raised an eyebrow and it was as if he'd opened a flood-gate as ideas washed over her. She shook her head to clear it. 'I need to focus on the hotel's restaurant first. If I do a good job there, then...' She swallowed, a new kind of excitement spiking through her. 'Then I guess we'll see.'

'You'll do a good job, Bella.'

She wished she had his confidence, but if effort counted for anything then she *would* pull this off.

His eyes were as blue as the ocean outside the window and as warm as the spring sunshine. She swallowed. 'I'm sorry I said you had no heart. That wasn't true.'

Their eyes locked and something shimmered between them. It created a disturbance in the air, like a heat haze. She saw then that, where there'd been two sofa-cushions' distance be-tween them, now there was only one and she wasn't sure which of them had moved.

Hunger flared in his eyes. It softened her belly, her womb. He made as if to reach out and touch her. She swayed towards him, aching for his touch.

And then he slammed back in his seat. 'Don't go getting all starry-eyed on me, Bella.'

Her heart thumped painfully. She sat back, too. 'Starry-eyed over you?' She made herself snort. 'You have tickets on your-self.' She tossed her hair. 'You think you are such a player, but you aren't even in the game, buster!'

He grinned. 'That's better.'

'Pah!' She struggled to hide a smile of her own. 'What's more, you can't even make a decent coffee.'

She grabbed their mugs and made for the kitchen. She

ground coffee beans, stared out at the harbour and told her wilful body to behave. Dominic was right—stars in her eyes were the last thing she needed.

Juggling briefcase and file, Bella let herself into the apartment. Late-afternoon light poured in at the windows and not for the first time she was grateful that her father had changed their temporary living quarters.

She might not be any less aware of Dominic here than at the previous apartment, but at least they had room to breathe here, and room to work.

She moved out of the tiny foyer and pulled up short when she saw Dominic seated at the dining table with his back to her. He didn't turn to greet her and that was when she realised he hadn't heard her. For some reason that made her smile.

That table could comfortably serve four people as a desk, and every evening for the past two weeks they'd set up at it and Dominic had taught her all he'd promised to—spreadsheets, budgets, basic and not-so-basic accounting.

Plus more. He'd taught her how to recognise her staff's strengths and, as a result, how to delegate tasks efficiently. He'd taught her that she didn't have to do it all on her own. Most importantly of all, he'd instilled a new sense of confidence in her. He'd made her realise that she did have a brain that was worth a whole lot more than a tuppence. He'd even taught her long division.

He'd been patient, incisive and knowledgeable and she'd developed a whole new respect for him.

She went to greet him, but…

What was he doing?

A grin broke through her when she realised he was dangling a piece of string from the table to the floor and, although Minky was doing her best to feign indifference, she obviously hadn't fooled Dominic for a moment.

Bella set her briefcase on the floor. He showed the same patience with Minky as he had with her when explaining a difficult concept. She held her file against her chest and watched. Minky stood, stretched and ambled in a disinterested circle, but when she sat again she was closer to the piece of string than before. It made Bella grin. She wanted to tell Minky to stop the pretence and give in now. Dominic would win her around in the end. Resistance would be futile.

And then Minky pounced. Dominic laughed and twitched the string just out of reach. Minky danced, arched her back, pounced, ran away and then came racing back to pounce again. The cat's utter delight in the game made Bella grin. No wonder Mel adored the cat. But it was Dominic's low rumble of a laugh and his enjoyment that made something in her chest catch. He would make such a great dad!

The thought was so unexpected it made her blink, but in the next breath her shoulders started to ache as if a heavy weight bore down on them. Dominic claimed he didn't believe in love. He swore he would never marry, would never commit to a woman, would never have a family. Couldn't he see how much he'd be missing?

Sadness for him welled inside her. Sadness for the loneliness, the isolation in which he wrapped himself. She must've made some betraying noise because he swung around and then gave an abashed grin. 'Sprung, I see.'

'Totally.' Her voice came out husky. 'Admit it, you like the cat.'

'She's grown on me.'

His red-gold hair haloed his head, his eyes sparked blue and it suddenly hit Bella that a great part of her sadness was for herself too—because she wanted to grow on him, as well?

She moistened her lips, told herself to stop being ridiculous and forced herself to move more fully into the room. 'Coffee?'

'I'd love one.'

She dropped her file to the table as she walked past, bent down to pet Minky and dragged in the scent of cinnamon, wishing she had the right to drop a kiss to the top of Dominic's head so she could breathe him in more fully. 'You should get yourself a dog,' she said when she straightened.

'I live in an apartment.'

'So? Get a house instead.'

'Dogs aren't conducive to a jet-setting lifestyle.'

Neither was a wife and children. Bella forced herself around the bench. She peered over the top of it at him for a moment and shrugged. 'So? Get a dog-sitter.'

She promptly set about grinding coffee beans. 'Or get a life,' she murmured under her breath. A proper life. A life filled with people, passion, fun, laughter and…

Stop it! How he chose to live his life was none of her business. Why should she be sad that he cut himself off from the things she thought vital?

She swallowed, her mouth suddenly dry.

Why did she make sure there was always citrus tart in the refrigerator? Citrus tart wasn't her weakness, it was his. Her hands started to shake. Why did she spend the week thinking of some fun social thing they could do together on the weekends and was then on cloud nine when he enjoyed it and praised her inventiveness?

She crossed her arms, her fingers digging into the flesh above her elbows. For heaven's sake, why had she looked forward to learning long division?

Dominic made her laugh. He challenged her. He made her a better person.

She glanced at him and her heart thumped hard. She was in a right pickle. She'd gone and done the most ridiculous thing a girl could do.

CHAPTER TWELVE

'BELLA?'

Concern flared in Dominic's eyes. Bella shook herself and forced a smile to her lips. 'You know, I do want a dog and I don't want a jet-setting lifestyle.'

He didn't say anything.

'I love my father, but I don't want to spend the next ten years working for his company if it means spending two months in this capital city, and then three months in a different capital city, until all of those capital cities start blurring into each other and I find it harder and harder to be passionate about any location. I want to run my own restaurant. Just the one. I don't need world domination. I want to stay in one place and...'

'And?'

And have a family. But her throat had closed over, making it impossible to say out loud. She wanted to have a family.

She'd always wanted to have a family, but it was a dream that she'd told herself was for the future and not for the here and now. She'd kept telling herself that she was too young, but...

The two budding relationships she'd had that could've developed into something more, she'd sabotaged. Dominic had been right; she did use her virginity as a shield. She hadn't been able to face the thought that either man might find her lacking, that they might think her ignorant and feeble-minded.

Her mouth dried as she reached for two coffee mugs. She'd

shared her fears with Dominic and he hadn't laughed at her, he hadn't thought any the less of her. He still had faith in her. That had changed something inside her on a deep and fundamental level.

She wanted to have a family. And she didn't want to put that dream off any more.

She glanced across at him and could imagine how her dream would repel him. She wanted to have a family and it was pointless denying it any longer: she ached to have that family with Dominic. It was stupid. It was crazy and futile.

And she couldn't do anything about it.

'And what else do you want, Bella?'

She swallowed, but smiling was beyond her. 'I want to grow roots somewhere. I want to belong to a community.'

'I guess you won't be working on the next Maldini hotel, then?'

Was there a hint of sadness in the beach-blue of his eyes? She dismissed the notion as wishful thinking. 'I guess that gig is all yours.' It would be wiser to face the truth, to not spin unrealistic fantasies. 'I think Papa will understand. I think he'll be proud of me anyway.'

'I'm sure of it, Bella.'

Why did he have to say her name like that—as if he liked saying it? It thickened her throat all over again.

She poured one of the coffees down the sink and set the other in front of him. He raised an eyebrow when he saw she didn't have one. 'I changed my mind. I need a walk to blow away the cobwebs rather than a coffee.'

She headed to her room to change into jeans and sneakers and prayed he wouldn't suggest coming along. She needed time away from him for a bit. She had to work out exactly what she needed to do.

Did she fight for Dominic? Or did she let him go without a murmur?

* * *

Bella sat on a sand dune on Nobby's beach and tried to verbalise her options. 'One.' She held out a finger. 'I could tell him how I feel.'

She snorted. Yeah, right, as if that wouldn't have him running for the hills. She barely suppressed a shudder when she imagined his reaction.

'Two.' She held out a second finger. 'I could just continue on as if nothing has changed, hide my feelings and do absolutely nothing.'

She fell back on the sand to stare up at the late-afternoon sky. The clouds were tinged pink and orange, the sky a pale blue. Do nothing? Everything inside her protested at the thought. Energy seeped out until she thought she might melt into the sand. Do nothing?

'What else can I do?' she asked the clouds. To tell him how she felt would make him miserable. She didn't want to make him feel bad about himself. It wasn't his fault she'd fallen in love with him. He'd warned her about the kind of man he was, of the kind of life he wanted.

They'd agreed they were chalk and cheese, oil and water, seriously unsuited. To tell him how she felt wouldn't change a thing. It wouldn't magically bring him round to her way of thinking. It'd only make things awkward.

She slapped the sand. In love with Dominic? When had it happened?

She didn't ask why; the why was easy. Chalk and cheese, oil and water, had nothing to do with it. Nor did the tempting breadth of his shoulders, the tantalising blue of his eyes or the impact of his smile.

It had everything to do with the inner man. She'd watched him befriend Minky, she'd witnessed his gentleness towards the men at the shelter—even as they brought back bad memories for him. She'd seen how hard he worked, how he encouraged his staff and how important it was for him to do a good job for Marco. Regardless of what he said and thought about himself, Dominic was an honourable man.

He worked hard, he played hard and he could make her laugh as easily as he could do long division. His presence made her feel more alive than she had ever felt in her life before.

How would she live without it when this project was over?

She pressed her hands to the cool of the sand. One thing she couldn't fool herself about was that Dominic returned her feelings.

Or that he ever would.

She sat up and stared out to sea. She had no right to expect anything from him.

A small breeze whipped up, loosening strands of hair from her ponytail and tossing them about her face. She hugged her sweatshirt more tightly about her. There was one thing she and Dominic did have, though—chemistry.

Ha! As if…

She stilled in the act of trying to get her hair back under control. Chemistry… Making love…

No, she couldn't!

Her blood started to pound. More hair escaped the grip of her ponytail. Well, why not?

Stop it! She wanted to make love to a man she meant to spend the rest of her life with.

She wanted to make love to the man she loved. Right or wrong, it was as simple as that.

Blood surged around every part of her body, firing her with an ancient energy and a primitive longing. She dug her arms up to her elbows in the sand in an effort to anchor herself.

Dominic didn't do 'for ever', but that didn't mean she couldn't store up as many memories of him as she could before they went their separate ways. They could have one fabulous night together.

Couldn't they?

It was possible, wasn't it?

Her heart surged against her ribs. She shook her arms free and reached up to pull the band from her hair. She tossed her head to free her locks to the caress of the wind. She wanted to love the man she first made love to.

She loved Dominic.

To make love with him… Her breath caught. The idea might be the wildest one she'd had yet, the most daring, but in her heart it felt right.

He would resist any attempts at intimacy. Despite all he said, he was honourable at heart.

She leapt to her feet. She'd just have to find a way to overcome his resistance; that was all there was to it.

The moment Dominic pushed through the front door his mouth started to water. Whatever Bella was cooking, it smelt sensational.

Bella emerged from behind the bench that separated the kitchen from the rest of the living room. She sent him a smile so brilliant it pulled his skin tight across his bones. 'Hello.'

Alarm bells went off in his head, just like that. 'What are you so dressed up for?' he barked.

She blinked. Her chin lifted. 'Hello, Bella, how was work today?'

Her pointed reproach made him feel suddenly graceless and awkward. 'Sorry.'

'Besides, I'm not all that dressed up.'

She shrugged. It drew his attention to her shoulders. The neckline of her blouse was modest, but her shoulders were bare. All of that delectable olive skin on display made his mouth dry. Then he noticed the dining table. It was set with white linen and crystal. What on earth? 'You're more dressed up than usual,' he ground out. He nodded at the table set for two. 'Are you expecting company?'

She planted her hands on her hips and stuck one of those hips out. It made him realise precisely how long her legs were.

It made his mouth more arid than a desert. He wanted to croak 'Water,' only he knew how absurd that would sound.

'No, I am not expecting company. House rules, remember? No entertaining in the apartment.'

His tie loosened from around his throat as the relief hit him. She didn't have a date? No one was coming over? It was just the two of them? The world righted itself again.

The two of them? His tie promptly threatened to cut off his circulation.

He found it difficult not to stare at her. The filmy orange of her blouse highlighted the rich darkness of her hair and her eyes, while the flirty pink material of her skirt skimmed her hips to float about her knees. If a breeze caught hold of that skirt…

He shut his eyes and counted to three. He opened them again. 'So this is all in honour of…?' He tried to keep his voice steady.

'I found out today that one of our diners means to propose to his girlfriend on opening night. He came in today to ask if we could create a special menu for them.'

She'd said yes, of course. He could see that in her eyes. He grinned and shook his head. She was such a romantic.

'So this—' she turned to gesture to the set table, the kitchen, her clothes '—is to help me find the right mood for our courting couple.'

Dear God in heaven. Her back was bare! The tension ratcheted back through him with ten times the intensity.

'Why don't you put your briefcase and laptop away for the day, shower and change, and then come and give me your opinion of the meal I've prepared?'

That was when he realised he hadn't moved from his spot just inside the door. He hadn't moved from the first moment he'd clapped eyes on her. He should say no. He should make some excuse and get the hell out of there. Plead work…

She twirled a loose strand of hair in one finger, vulnerability flashing across her face. 'I'd really welcome your feedback, Dominic. I want to get this just right.'

He couldn't refuse the entreaty in her eyes. It'd take a much colder heart than his to do so. 'Uh, right.' He forced his legs forward and then realised he was going in the wrong direction. 'Will do.' He changed direction with what he hoped was finesse. 'Shower. Right. Good idea.'

It'd be a cold shower.

And he'd change into jeans to keep it deliberately casual. He shut his bedroom door and sagged against it. This meal wasn't for him, he reminded himself. He'd tell her the food was superb, and the mood perfect, and then he'd promptly set his laptop up at the end of the table and immerse himself in work. Business, that was all this was—business. He tapped his fingers to his head in an attempt to burn it on to his brain.

He nearly forgot it when he entered the living room again fifteen minutes later. Bella had dimmed the lights. She'd lit candles. She'd created an intimate, sexy atmosphere in all the light and airy space of the living room. He wanted to growl that none of this was necessary, blow out all the candles and turn the lights back on.

He pinched the bridge of his nose. *Get a grip.* She's an artist. She was experimenting, practising at creating someone's dream. His hormones were his problem, not hers.

She came to stand beside him to survey the table. The faint tang of lemon and some herb, freshly cut, filled his nostrils, firing him with renewed awareness of her.

'What do you think?'

Her voice was low, hushed. It whispered across his skin like a promise. He swallowed. 'It looks great, Bella. Beautiful.' She was beautiful.

She turned, her eyes warm, her generous lips lifting. 'Thank you.'

Her pleasure at his simple compliment touched him.

She'd pulled her hair up onto the top of her head in a kind of sexy knot with loose strands spilling down around her face and neck. She twined one long tendril of hair around her finger now, drawing his eyes to the sleek line of her neck. Pure temptation and she didn't even realise it. He tried to banish the images that flooded him: of the way her neck would arch as he pressed kisses to it; of the softness of her curves as they pressed against him; of the warmth of her skin as he traced lazy circles against the bare skin of her back.

'I hope you're hungry.'

He snapped back. Her eyes had become huge in her face. He cursed himself for all but undressing her with his eyes. 'Starved,' he croaked.

He had to get a handle on himself and the situation. He couldn't fall under the spell of the fantasy she was weaving. Bella was a virgin. In her mind, this evening was innocent. She didn't know she was playing with fire. If he followed his natural urges and made love to her, he'd make her cry.

Bile burned his tongue.

If he slept with Bella she'd weave fantasies about him in her mind. No woman should do that. He set his jaw. He would not make Bella cry. She deserved her dream of a happy-ever-after with her prince. And if that didn't work out for her? He rolled his shoulders. Well, he refused to be the guy who shattered her dreams and disillusioned her.

She touched his arm and he had to bite back a groan. 'Have a seat.' With that she moved into the kitchen. He forced wooden legs to the table, forced himself to sit when all he wanted to do was drag her into his arms.

She came back carrying two plates and set one in front of him.

Oysters? *God, no!* He stared at the six oyster shells arranged in a circle in front of him. He cleared his throat. *Business.* 'I take it our foolish young swain has given you a complete list of his beloved's likes and dislikes?'

'Oh, yes.'

Her rich deep chuckle did nothing to ease the heat washing through him.

'And one very simple instruction.'

He clenched his hands in his napkin before placing it on his lap and smoothing it out. 'Which is?'

She lifted one of the oysters and sipped it straight out of its shell. The sight nearly knocked him out his chair. 'Seduction,' she murmured.

His groin swelled. He adjusted it in his lap before it cut off circulation to his brain entirely.

'That's the mood he wants me to create.' She sent him a heavy-lidded smile, her lips full and her eyes dreamy. 'How am I doing so far?'

She had the seduction thing nailed. He straightened and shoved his shoulders back. 'You do know you aren't going to be the one sitting across the table from him?'

She merely smiled and glanced at his plate. 'I thought you said you were hungry. I've prepared the oysters in three different ways. You have to try at least one of each.'

She lifted another shell to her lips and he dragged his gaze away. Eating had to be far easier than watching her practise the art of seduction. He gulped down three oysters in quick succession. Man, they were good. He devoured the rest.

'Well?'

Her eyes lowered to his lips. Didn't she have any idea of the effect she was having on him? He wanted to fall to his knees and cry, 'Uncle!'

'Which did you prefer?'

He swallowed, stared at his plate and then pointed wildly at one of the shells.

'Mmm.' Her tongue ran along her bottom lip. All the way along. 'I liked that one, too.'

Just when he was starting to think that she was being deliberately provocative, that she was purposely teasing him, taunting him, stretching him to his limits, she rose. 'Would you open the champagne while I serve up the next course?'

She disappeared back behind the long bench to the kitchen. He scraped a hand down his face, pressing his fingertips against his eyelids and dragged in deep breaths. He didn't open the champagne. With his eyes closed he didn't see her come back to the table, but he smelt her; heard the swishing slide of her flirty little skirt; could practically feel her warmth steal across his skin from across the other side of the table. She dredged his senses with her very essence.

Her soft, womanly and sharp chef smells swirled around him—a combination of roses, fried onions and lemons. He didn't know how such a combination could fire his senses to life. He didn't know how such a combination could be so sexy. Maybe it wouldn't have been on another woman, but it was sexy as hell on Bella.

The feel of her so near sent a frisson of electricity racing up his bare arms and under the sleeves of his polo shirt to tighten his nipples. He forced his arms off the table and straightened his back.

She slid a plate in front of him. 'You look like you need an early night,' she said, her words soft and husky.

'Sounds good,' he managed. If only she knew how good.

'Sure does,' she sighed.

Her words held a promise he could hardly make himself believe. A swift glance at her face told him nothing.

'Do you like lobster?'

He stared down at his plate. Long, thick slabs of lobster meat were arranged strategically along with three shallow bowls of dipping sauce. 'Are you *deliberately* trying to make the food look suggestive?' The words barked out of him. He sucked in a breath. A more experienced woman would've realised by now exactly the effect she was having on him.

Only, no woman had ever affected him the way Bella did.

She took her seat and turned wide eyes to him. 'Of course I am. It's part of the game.'

It didn't feel like a game. Not any more.

She picked up a piece of lobster meat and carefully covered its tip in a creamy sauce, drawing it back and forth through the dish. Sauce trickled down its length when she righted it again;

she caught it with the pink tip of her tongue before it reached her fingers. Then she ran her tongue up its length with a slow relish that caught his breath and refused to give it back, firing his imagination with forbidden images of that sweet, pink tongue on his own turgid flesh.

Her eyes speared his and in that instant he knew she wanted him. Whatever other excuse she'd given, this meal—this seductive, heady meal—was entirely for his benefit. All he had to do was reach across the table, draw her to her feet and she would be his. Ready, willing and eager.

Heat licked his veins. To take Bella to his bed? He couldn't think of anything that would give him more pleasure. He couldn't think of anything he wanted more, that he had ever wanted more.

He stared into those eyes as desire and rationality warred with each other. A man could lose himself in those eyes, in fantasies built around those lips. A man could lose his soul, his everything…including his freedom. There would be a price to pay if he slept with Bella.

That thought didn't dampen the desire firing though him. It didn't ease the persistent ache in his groin. It did give him the momentary strength to drag his eyes from hers, to ease himself back in his chair a fraction.

He would not give up his freedom. Bella was a 'for ever' kind of woman. He wasn't a 'for ever' kind of anything—not where women were concerned. He was lucky to commit to the day after tomorrow.

He wasn't even prepared to get a dog.

Yes, there'd be a price to pay if he slept with Bella, but it wouldn't be him paying the piper, it'd be her. She'd pay with her dreams and with her disillusion. He wished to hell that wasn't the case, that Bella was one of those sophisticated beauties who could take casual affairs in their stride, but she wasn't. And he was self-aware enough to know that, if she were, he probably wouldn't ache for her with this level of intensity.

Damn it! She was like a bad case of the chicken pox. They

itched so bad they nearly sent you out of your mind, but you knew if you scratched them they'd scar you for life.

'Dominic?'

He dragged his gaze back to hers. 'Do you know what the hell you're doing?'

She smiled. It was low, wide and sexy as hell. Her eyes sparked with anticipation. 'Of course I know what I'm doing, Dominic.' The words came out on short quick breaths. 'I'm trying to seduce you. How am I doing?'

For a moment her eyes shimmered with vulnerability, as if she thought she might be going about the seduction thing the wrong way, and it was almost his undoing. He forced himself to push away from the table. 'This can't happen.'

Bella fought back the panic that blocked her throat when she glimpsed the resolution in Dominic's eyes. What had she done wrong? She'd planned everything to the tiniest detail—what she'd wear, the food she'd serve, the wine, the smoky jazz music that crooned in the background. She'd even locked Minky up in her bedroom.

Dominic's eyes had lit up in appreciation the moment he'd first seen her. He'd told her the table setting was beautiful. He'd complimented the entrée, and all the while he'd practically devoured her with his eyes. He wanted her. She might be a virgin but she knew that much.

'What did I do wrong?' she demanded as he stalked across to flick on the light switch. The room was instantly flooded with light; so much for evocative candlelight.

He scratched both hands back through his hair until it stood on end. She ached to smooth it back down. 'You didn't do anything wrong.'

That was when she noticed how tightly he held himself and hope lifted through her. Dominic's control was hanging by a thread. She could still snap it yet.

She'd need to tread carefully, though.

First, she needed to put him at ease again.

'Fine, so it's not going to happen. Will you let Minky out of my bedroom?' She leaned across and blew out the candles. She kicked off her shoes and retrieved a jug of cold water and two glasses from the kitchen. 'But we can at least eat the food, can't we?'

He hovered nearby, clearly uncertain. He let the cat out; Minky bolted straight over to Bella and started to meow imperiously. 'Of course there's some lobster for you, too, Princess Minky-Moo,' she crooned, placing a little lobster meat onto her bread-and-butter plate and setting it down on the floor for the cat.

She glanced up at Dominic as she unrolled her napkin and spread it across her lap. 'The food cost a bomb. Don't make me feed it all to Minky.'

She picked up her knife and fork—no more eating with her fingers—and started to cut into the tender chunks of lobster meat and eat it. She closed her eyes, chewed and swallowed. 'Man.' She opened her eyes and shook her head. 'This is really good. The seafood in Newcastle is exquisite.'

With something that sounded a lot like a curse, Dominic stalked over and took his seat again. Bella concentrated on her food and did her best to barely glance across at the man opposite. But she was aware of his heat, his scent and the tight defensive set of his shoulders.

She needed them to be relaxed. She needed *him* to be relaxed and with his guard down before she hit him with round two.

Stickability? She snorted. By the end of the evening he wouldn't doubt her determination ever again.

'What?' he said in answer to her snort.

Keep it light, she ordered. She had to keep it light. 'You know what our foolish swain wanted to do?'

'What?'

He stared at her with narrowed eyes, almost as if waiting for her to pounce. She grinned. Pouncing was one tactic, she supposed, but it did lack a certain polish and sophistication.

Still, it did have a primitive appeal. She wondered what he'd do if she did.

'The foolish swain, Bella?'

She snapped to. 'He wanted me to make up some kind of berry-fool concoction with the engagement ring embedded within the dessert.'

He stared. 'Bad idea?'

She rolled her eyes. 'Well, hello, yes! Besides the hygiene issue of ensuring the ring is clean and won't contaminate the food, what if she swallowed the ring, or cracked a tooth when she bit into it?'

His lips twitched a fraction and a thread of fire twisted through her belly.

'I could see how a trip to the emergency department might put a dampener on the romantic mood,' he allowed.

'Exactly. And, even if she does find said ring without incident, it's going to be covered in cream, custard, berry coulis and—' she gave a strategic shudder '—that's just a bit too icky.'

His lips twitched some more. 'Icky?'

'Yes, it's a very precise kitchen term.'

He laughed. The fire in her belly arced lower and deeper. They finished the lobster and the accompanying salad.

'You know,' she said, lining up her knife and fork and pushing her plate away, 'some people seem to do the most extreme and outrageous things when they're proposing.'

Dominic wiped his fingers on his napkin. He had long fingers and beautiful hands. 'Like?'

She dragged her gaze from his hands to shrug. 'Oh, you know, by proposing on national television in front of thousands of viewers.'

'Another bad move?'

'Well, I'd hate it. It smacks of blackmail—no woman could have the heart to turn down a guy on national television et cetera. She'd be vilified by an entire nation if she said no. Embarrassment factor—high. Romantic factor—low.' She collected up their plates. 'Dessert? I made choc-dipped strawberries but they've lost their appeal for the moment. There's chocolate mud cake and citrus tart in the fridge.'

'Citrus tart,' he said promptly. He gestured to the champagne that he hadn't opened. 'Would you still like me to do the honours?'

She shook her head. 'I'll pop it back in the fridge for another time, unless you'd like a glass?'

'No, no.' He handed her the bottle.

She wanted a clear head for the moment. They could save the champagne and strawberries for later, for post-seduction. She hid a secret smile as she placed a slice of citrus tart onto a dessert plate.

'What about sky-writing a proposal of marriage?'

She returned with their desserts and sat and spooned a forkful of mud cake into her mouth as she considered his question. Finally she nodded. 'Yeah, that's nice. It shows thought and it's a big gesture, but you could still keep the moment private just between the two of you.'

Dominic cut off an enormous mouthful of citrus tart and groaned as he ate it. He pointed to his plate. 'Do you know how good this is?'

Everything inside her clenched in need. She wanted him to look at her like that. She seized her glass of iced water and drained it dry.

She loved him so much, wanted him so much. It scared her to think what it would be like to leave here in a couple of weeks' time, to leave him. It might be insane to want to spend one passionate night with Dominic, but she knew it would be a memory that she could cling on to for a lifetime.

She had a feeling it would be a memory that would help her through the terrible loneliness and longing of the coming months. She already knew that they would be terrible, knew it in her bones. Knew it in her heart. She set her fork down, unable to eat any more mud cake.

'How would you like to be proposed to, Bella?'

Her heart leapt. She told it to stop being stupid. Dominic's question was purely hypothetical. He was making conversation in an effort to stave off any awkwardness.

'Well, ideally it would have to involve champagne.'

'French, naturally?'

'But of course.'

He grinned and pointed to her plate. 'And chocolate mud cake?'

'Yes, please. This is my fantasy after all, right?'

'Right.'

She cocked her head to one side. 'I wouldn't need anything showy or big.'

'Except for the champagne,' he said gravely.

'Which would have to be French,' she repeated with equal gravity. And then they both laughed. 'So, a picnic on a deserted beach would fit the bill nicely. Champagne, chocolate mud cake, perhaps some strawberries and…' She trailed off with a shrug.

'And then he'd pop the magic question?'

She shook her head. 'He'd have to tell me why he loved me first so that I could believe he meant it.'

Dominic stared, a spoonful of citrus tart halted halfway to his mouth. 'What would he say?'

'I have no idea,' she confessed. 'But it would be heartfelt and true.' Then she folded her arms and winked at him. 'And it better be good.'

Dominic laughed, as she'd meant him to. She wasn't silly enough to imagine that scenario with him. He did know that, didn't he?

Every muscle she had stiffened. *He didn't know that!*

She leaned towards him. 'Dominic, I wasn't imagining any kind of happy-ever-after with you, you know. I just wanted one night of passion.'

He choked.

'Did you think I had our first-born's name already picked out?' She sat back and shook her head. 'So *that's* what I did wrong, huh? I didn't make my intentions plain enough.'

Dominic continued to choke. Her confidence wavered. 'Or did I do something else wrong, too?'

She poured him a glass of water. He gulped half of it down. 'Bella, like I already said, you didn't do anything wrong.'

'Oh, please!' She pushed her plate away. 'If I'd got it right you'd be putty in my hands by now.'

All the tension shot back into his body. She thought he might splutter his ice water across the table. 'Bella!'

'But you're not putty and I'm seriously disappointed about that. I'm a girl who likes to learn from her mistakes. So?'

The pulse at the base of his jaw pounded. 'If I didn't know you as well as I do, we'd probably be tearing each other's clothes off as we speak, but—'

'Sounds good to me. In fact, it sounds great!' She didn't try to hide her sudden breathlessness.

'But I do know you.'

It took a moment for his words to sink in. When they did, she flinched. There was a whole level of pain she hadn't experienced yet. Her total vulnerability to this man appalled her, but there was nothing she could do about it.

'Don't look like that,' he groaned.

'You tell me you don't like me enough to make love with me? How am I supposed to look?'

'It's not because I don't like you!' he shouted. 'It's because I like you too much!'

She blinked.

'You call it making love—I call it sex. At the moment your hormones are going wild, but tomorrow or the day after you'd regret the impulse. You'd regret having sex with me. I don't want to be responsible for that.'

She wouldn't regret it. She knew that as well as she knew her recipe for chocolate mud cake off by heart. 'I'm not building fantasies about you, Dominic. I'm not dreaming we'll make love and suddenly you'll be transformed into a prince who'll declare his undying love for me and propose to me at sunset on a beach.'

He stared. 'Sunset? You never said anything about a sunset.'
'It's a work in progress,' she shot back.

And he had another thing coming if he thought he could deflect her. She stood. She walked around the table to him. He stood, too. He didn't back away, but she could see by the tensing of his muscles how tightly he held himself in check.

She reached out and placed her hand on his chest. Beneath her palm, his heart pounded. 'I have never in my life wanted a man the way I want you, Dominic. You make me breathe harder just by looking at me.' His heart pounded harder against her hand. 'You touch me and for some reason my entire body comes alive. Colours and scents become sharper and clearer, but at the same time the rest of the world recedes. I want to make love with you. I want to know how truly amazing one night with you would be. I don't want your promises. I just want your touch and your body, Dominic.'

He stilled. A great sigh juddered out of him. His heartbeat continued to pound against her palm and a thrill shot through her. He seized her chin in his fingers and forced her gaze to his. Her breath caught. He was going to kiss her!

He bent his head; her lips opened in anticipation, her eyelids fluttered closed…

'Open your eyes,' he ordered.

She did.

He peered into them with a brutal relentlessness that took her off-guard. He peered into her very soul with a merciless efficiency that stripped her bare and unveiled all her secrets. In panic, she tried to remove her chin from his grip, but he refused to release her. And there was nowhere to look except into his eyes.

And she felt the exact moment he discovered the secret she most wanted to keep. She felt it in the shudder that wracked his body, felt it in the way his fingers tightened about her chin, and then in the way he let her go. Felt it in the space that yawned between them as he stepped away. Saw it in the shocked blue of his eyes and the momentary slackness of his jaw.

'No,' he choked out.

She couldn't lie about it; she wouldn't. 'It's true.' She shrugged and tried to smile.

He flinched and swore.

'So you see? It's already too late. Whether we make love or not, Dominic, I've already fallen in love with you.'

He stabbed a finger at her. 'That wasn't supposed to happen.'

She shrugged. 'I don't have any expectations of you.' Then she stuck out a hip, planted her hand on it and hitched up her chin. 'Oh, except for a night or three of pleasure.'

For a moment she almost thought he'd smile. Hope surged through her—hope, anticipation and a breaking heart.

Dominic's hand snaked around the back of her head and he pulled her in close. His lips slammed to her in a hard kiss—a thorough, plundering kiss that sent the blood surging through her veins and fire licking across the surface of her skin.

He broke off and pressed his forehead to hers. 'I'm sorry, Bella. I never meant to hurt you.'

Fear froze her at the look in his eye. 'I know that,' she whispered. 'It's not your fault.' It wasn't anybody's fault, but she doubted he heard her. He was already striding away. Her heart burned so hard she had to clench her hands to stop from doubling over. 'Where are you going?' she choked out.

'To pack my things. I'm moving out. I'll see you on Monday.'

Bella sat at the table amid the ruin that was their dinner and watched him slam into his bedroom. Rather than one splendid night with Dominic, she'd driven him away.

The click of the apartment door closing a short while later echoed in her heart. He hadn't even said goodbye.

CHAPTER THIRTEEN

THE grand opening night for the Newcastle Maldini was going exactly to plan. Dominic knew that Bella had visualised tonight down to the minutest detail and as he moved through the crowd he couldn't imagine that she was anything but elated beyond measure.

All the beautiful people of Newcastle and farther abroad were here. The restaurant and bar areas, lounge and foyer, were filled with glittering patrons milling, talking, mixing and being seen. He'd received a multitude of compliments about the décor, the grandeur of the foyer with its stunning chandelier, the comfort and luxury of the guest rooms, and for the efficiency and pleasantness of the staff.

Not to mention the food. There'd been a lot of praise for the food. The diners in the restaurant were literally gushing with tributes. It couldn't be denied that the restaurant was the unofficial hub for this evening's festivities and Dominic could clearly see why. Bella and her staff had created a sophisticated and stylish dining room which was the most inviting space in the hotel.

The entire project was a *tour de force*. Something inside Dominic lifted when he glanced across the room at Marco. The older man could not keep the grin from his face. His evident pleasure, his almost childlike delight, was the highlight of Dominic's evening. He knew it would be Bella's, as well.

So why the hell wasn't he beaming, too? Why was he finding it so hard to keep a smile on his face?

He glanced at Bella—again. He'd given up counting the number of times his eyes sought her out. As the restaurant's hostess this evening, she'd stolen his breath. She wore a fitted black lace dress, black tights and killer heels that highlighted the length of her glorious legs. Her dress moulded to her curves, emphasising her lethal hourglass figure. All that womanly perfection made his mouth dry and an ache start up somewhere deep inside.

It wasn't her beauty, though, that had charmed the restaurant's patrons. It was her warmth. She moved through the restaurant with unhurried ease. She seemed to anticipate her diners' every need before they did. It was obvious that her most important goal for the evening was that her diners enjoy themselves.

Her staff responded to her directions with respect and eagerness, and he noted that she was quick to praise them, too. In fact, he noted every damn thing about her.

His hands clenched. Wherever Bella moved she radiated charm, and unaffected hospitality. That was, she radiated them to everyone except him. His lips twisted. Twice he'd spoken to her this evening. He'd wanted to tell her how exquisite the restaurant looked. He'd wanted to tell her what an outstanding job she'd done.

She'd listened politely, she'd thanked him politely and then she'd moved on. Her distance rankled. He missed the shared jokes, the banter and teasing. He missed her enthusiasm for everything except mornings.

Hell, he missed living with her.

You were the idiot who moved out of the apartment.

He'd had to.

He turned and headed back towards the bar area, away from the restaurant and Bella. He did another circuit of the lounge and foyer, spoke to the VIPs, flirted with the socialites, but inevitably he ended up back at the restaurant. It drew him as an unguarded plate of food called to a stray dog that hadn't eaten in several days.

Marco waved him over to his table. Dominic answered the summons with alacrity. 'Where are your dinner companions?' He gestured to the empty table.

'They've deserted me to sample the delights of the bar and the lounge. They tell me they mean to report back to me in an hour with their opinions. Now sit, sit,' he ordered. He waved a waiter over. 'Champagne please, young Robert.' The fact that Marco knew his waiter's name made Dominic grin. Like father, like daughter. 'This one, if you please.' And he pointed to the most expensive bottle on the wine list.

'Very good, Mr Maldini.'

Marco's eyes danced. 'And will you tell my daughter I would like to see her?'

'Yes, sir.'

Bella was halfway across the room, and when the waiter spoke to her she turned and glanced at Marco's table. Her smile faltered for a moment when her eyes landed on Dominic. His heart burned in protest, but his blood kicked to life as she made her way towards them. She made slow progress as the people at nearly every table wanted to stop her and compliment her.

'Isn't my Bella beautiful?'

She was stunning! Dominic forced his gaze to his employer. 'She is a remarkable woman, Marco. She has done an amazing job here. You have every reason to be proud of her.'

'Yes.' Marco's brow momentarily darkened. 'So what the hell has happened between the pair of you? What have you done to her?'

'What have I—?'

They both broke off as the champagne arrived. And then Bella. At her father's urging, Bella sat, too. She took the seat closest to her father opposite Dominic. The candlelight danced across her face, turning her eyes to dark pools of mystery.

Marco did the honours with the champagne. He handed them each a glass. 'Dominic, Bella, you have made my dream a reality. You have exceeded all my expectations, all my wildest dreams. You have made me a very happy man.' He raised his glass. 'A toast to you both for all your hard work and brilliance. You have my gratitude and my admiration.'

They clinked glasses. Just for a moment Bella met his eyes, and Dominic's heart leapt into his throat. She glanced away, no smile lighting her face, and his heart slumped to his knees. His chest tightened, making it difficult to breathe. It took all his strength to force one sip of champagne down his throat.

He came to, to hear Marco say, 'You called the restaurant "Francine's"?'

'In honour of Mama.'

'She would be very proud of you, Bella. I am very proud of you.'

In the candlelight Dominic could see her eyes shimmer with unshed tears. She blinked hard a couple of times and he found his own throat thickening. She'd achieved what she'd set out to—Marco's respect and regard. He knew how much this moment meant to her. When she reached over to cover Marco's hand with hers, he saw that Marco had to blink hard, too.

'Papa, I want to thank you for being so patient with me these last few years, and I want to thank you for giving me this opportunity to prove myself. It means more to me than I can say.'

Marco gripped her hand. 'My Bella, all I want is for you to be happy. I have failed you so badly these last few years.'

Bella's jaw dropped. 'Failed me?'

'You have struggled to find your place in the world and I didn't know how to help you. Everything I did seemed to make things worse. Seemed to make you unhappy.'

Her mouth opened and closed. Finally she shook her head 'No, Papa, you didn't fail me.' Her eyes suddenly twinkled. 'But I think we need to work on our communication. I was only unhappy because I thought I was letting you down.'

Marco's jaw dropped. 'But...'

'No.' She held up a hand. 'Dominic made me see that I needed to prove to myself that I could do it, too.' She pulled in a breath. 'He was right.' She gestured around the restaurant. 'Yes, I wanted to make you proud of me, but I had to learn to be proud of myself, too. And I am.'

The glance and the tiny smile she sent across to him pierced Dominic to his marrow.

'I will always be grateful to you, Papa, for giving me this chance, and I will always be grateful to Dominic for so generously sharing his knowledge. I know what I want now and I know where I'm going. My future feels brighter because of my experiences here.'

Marco's face clouded over. 'Will you be going back to Italy and that restaurant you love so much? I understand if that's what you want but, my Bella, I will miss you.'

She leaned across and kissed his cheek. 'No, Papa. I want to stay in Australia and open my own restaurant.'

Marco's face lit up. He said something jubilant in Italian that suddenly made Dominic laugh.

Bella laughed, too. Then she sat back and sipped her wine. 'I'm afraid I'll be flying out to Italy on Monday, though.'

Marco nodded his head morosely. 'Yes, yes.'

Dominic stiffened. 'What? Why? We agreed to stay on for another week to ensure the handover of responsibilities goes without hiccup.'

'I have to make a cake.' Bella didn't look him in the eye. 'My cousin Immacolata's wedding is in a fortnight and something has gone wrong with the cake.'

Her natural generosity would've ensured that she'd offered her services and expertise to help.

'Be warned,' Marco muttered. 'Your aunt has a young man lined up for you.'

Bella laughed. 'Just the one?'

'No, three, but there's one in particular that she thinks you will like.'

Dominic's hands clenched. He wanted to punch someone. Bella with another man—laughing with another man, kissing him, making love with him, confessing her fears and dreams to him, building a life with him?

Whoa!

He physically pushed himself up and away from the table when he realised the direction his thoughts had taken. He wasn't a schmuck like his father. He didn't make a fool of himself over any woman.

Bella and Marco turned startled eyes to him. 'I, uh...' He pointed behind him. 'There's something I have to check.'

He stalked away, but there were too many people, too much noise. He needed to think. He pushed his way towards the staff domain of the kitchen.

Luigi glanced up when Dominic lurched through the doors. 'Mr Dominic, is everything all right?'

'Yes, yes.'

'Can I get you—?'

'I just need a moment of quiet,' he snapped as he made for the staff exit and the quiet of the night-lit alley. The ground beneath his feet swayed. He closed his eyes and breathed deeply.

He would not make a fool of himself over Bella. He would not become some spineless sap a woman could manipulate.

Bella said she loved you. She hasn't become a sap.

No, Bella was lovely and brave. Not a sap.

In that instant it finally hit him where Bella's love of life, her passion, came from: it came from loving. It came from caring about things. Lots of things: her father, her friends, Minky, homeless men, her cousin Immacolata... Yet each and every one of those things had the potential to hurt her.

Bella said she loved you. She hasn't become a sap.

He backed up to lean against the brick wall. He'd had the potential to hurt her. He clenched his hands. And he had.

But she hasn't become a sap!

The message the internal voice had been trying to beat into his brain finally impacted with his grey cells. For a moment everything inside him stilled, even his breath. Bella had told him she loved him and he'd walked away. But she hadn't collapsed into a heap. She hadn't sought him out during these last few weeks to cry or remonstrate with him, to try to change his mind. She'd acted professionally in their meetings. She'd held her head high. She'd maintained her dignity.

When are you going to realise you are not like your father?

He'd treated Bella the same way women had treated his father—with callousness. With coldness. And as a form of defence. But Bella hadn't collapsed into a heap the way his father always had.

He swallowed and tried to slow the whirling of his brain.

He didn't want to be like his father.

He didn't want to be like his father's ex-wives and girl-friends either.

And finally he could see there were alternatives. It wasn't an either-or situation. Something inside him started to lift.

He replayed his first meeting with Bella. He went over their ensuing arguments, her challenges, their laughter and their kiss. He thought back to the time before he knew Bella, to the boredom and the blankness. He stiffened with a curse. He might not be a sap, but he was an idiot!

He pushed away from the wall and shot back into the kitchen. 'Luigi?' he hollered, glancing around wildly for the other man.

'Yes, sir?' Luigi raced over. 'I'm here, Mr Dominic. Are you all right?'

'I…' He loved Bella. He wanted for ever with Bella. He had to win her, prove himself to her. 'Luigi, I need your help. I need a bottle of our finest champagne, some strawberries—' he grabbed the older man's shoulders '—hell, tell me there's chocolate mud cake left?'

'We have *Signorina* Bella's favourite.'

He sagged in relief and then held up two fingers. 'I need two slices and a picnic basket.'

'And glasses, plates and forks.'

He could've kissed the older man.

'A blanket too, perhaps?'

'Luigi, you are worth your weight in gold.'

The older man chuckled. 'No, no. But *Signorina* Bella is.'

Dominic didn't ask him how he knew. He paced impatiently while the basket was prepared and tried to work out exactly what he should say to Bella when he had her alone, but his mind refused to work.

Luigi handed him the picnic basket but kept a firm grip on it before Dominic could race away. 'You take good care of her, Mr Dominic.'

'I will,' he promised. He made a mental note to give the man a pay raise. Anyone who cared for Bella like that deserved good things.

'What on earth?'

Bella broke off, her throat closing over as Dominic approached her father's table. He strode towards her with a purpose that made her heart thump.

Don't be ridiculous. He'd made it clear—more than clear—where they stood. He halted in front of them. She nodded to the basket he held. 'All you need is a red cape,' she quipped, hoping wisecracks would keep the tears at bay. She would not let them fall until she was in bed alone tonight.

He reached down, captured her hand and pulled her to her feet. 'Marco, do you mind if I steal your daughter away for a bit?'

Marco grabbed the handle of the basket before Dominic could march off with her. 'You take good care of her.'

'I will, sir. I promise.'

She rolled her eyes. 'Don't I get any say in...?' Dominic

pulled her through the crowd and her words trailed off. He obviously had no intention of listening to a single word she said. She should pull him to a halt and snatch her hand from his, but she couldn't imagine making such a scene in front of all these people.

And a treacherous part of her didn't want to fight him. That stupid, treacherous part of her wanted to leave her hand in his and go with him wherever he led. For ever.

For ever? Ha! That wasn't going to happen.

And pretending it could, even for five minutes, would only lead to more heartbreak. So when he towed her outside through the giant carousel and into the cool of the evening air, she did pull him to a stop. 'Where are we going?'

'The beach.' He gestured to the beach below them, the sand silver in the starlight.

'Why?'

He urged her forward again. 'Why?' she demanded, doing her best to resist him.

'I need to talk to you.'

'Why can't we talk inside?'

'I want privacy.'

'But—'

He rounded on her, his eyes fierce. 'Do you want me to carry you?'

She pursed her lips. That could be kind of nice. He had shoulders to die for...

She cut the thought off. 'Fine,' she snapped. 'The beach.'

He didn't speak again, even once they reached the sand. He led her down to the deserted southern end of the beach. He spread out a picnic blanket. He took her hand and led her across to it and urged her to sit. He opened a bottle of champagne and poured her a glass. He spread strawberries onto a plate and set them in front of her. He served a slice of chocolate mud cake and handed it to her.

And then he paced up and down in front of her in the sand.

She stared at the goodies, she stared at him, and frowned. 'Um, Dominic, aren't you going to have anything?'

He swung to her. 'These are all your favourite things, right?'

'Yes, yes,' she assured him because it seemed so important to him. He stared pointedly at the plate she held so she forced herself to take a bite and couldn't stifle a groan of pure delight. 'Man, this stuff is good.'

She was starving! She'd been too keyed up to eat earlier and too busy afterwards to even think about food. She took another bite, wondering at the satisfaction that rippled across Dominic's features before he set to pacing again.

She held in a sigh. 'So let me guess. This is a thank-you for all my hard work and to celebrate our success, right?' He obviously wanted to be terribly adult about their relationship. She just wished they could drop the pretence and go their separate ways as quickly as they could.

Working day in and day out with Dominic had become a kind of torture and she wasn't a sadist. She'd come to realise that a quick and clean break would be for the best.

'This is about me not being a sap.'

Good Lord, where had that come from? She eyed him warily. 'Um, of course you're not.'

'I'm not like my father.'

She stilled. He stopped pacing to turn to her. 'I only realised that—' he glanced at his watch '—about fifteen minutes ago.'

'I...' She moistened her lips. She didn't know what to say. Being here with him like this was hell, but she didn't want to leave. Not now.

'You made me realise that, Bella.'

Her? How?

'And once I did, a whole string of epiphanies followed.'

They had?

'You told me you loved me but I walked away.'

She stared out at the water, at the path silvered by the moon, and swallowed hard, keeping her eyes unnaturally wide until the burning in them receded. When she was sure her voice would work she said, 'That's true.'

'But you maintained your dignity.'

Her head snapped up at that.

'That's something my father never managed.' He stared at her, his eyes two fierce points of light in the semi-darkness. 'But I am not like my father.'

Her heart started to beat hard. 'Why are you telling me this?'

He crouched down in front of her. 'So that you'll know, when I ask you in a minute to marry me, that I'm serious and that I mean it.'

Her piece of mud cake slid right off the plate to land on the blanket with a soft plop.

'Bella,' he chided. 'You're supposed to eat it, not drop it. Never mind, you can have my piece.' He scooped it off the blanket and back onto the plate and then grabbed a napkin to clean his hand and the blanket.

She watched him in a frozen haze. Finally she grabbed the napkin from his hand and tossed it somewhere behind her. She rose up on her knees to grab the lapels of his jacket and pull him down to the blanket beside her. 'What did you just say?' Her voice wobbled dangerously.

'I want to marry you. I love you, Bella, and I want you to know that I'm for real.'

Her chest and her throat grew too tight with the suspense, with the fear and the hope. She hauled in a breath and promptly burst into tears.

'Don't cry!' He rubbed her shoulders. 'Hell, Bella, I didn't mean to make you cry!'

The horror in his voice almost made her smile.

'Damn it!' His hands tightened around her shoulders. 'It's the sunset, isn't it? I didn't manage the sunset. The timing's all wrong and—'

'Shut up about the sunset,' she ordered through her tears, gulping her sobs back. She had far more important things to do at the moment than cry. 'Tell me why you love me. Make me believe you want to marry me.'

His face gentled. He traced a finger down her cheek. 'Bella, before I met you my life was blank, grey...monotonous.'

She tossed her head. 'You have a great job that you're brilliant at. How can that not be satisfying? You've slept with a lot of beautiful women. How could that be dull?'

'My high-flying career merely ensures that the wolf is never at my door again. It has nothing to do with filling a greater need or a passion. And the women...' He dragged a hand down his face. 'None of them touched my heart.'

He pulled his hand away, his eyes intense. 'And then I met you and I knew you had a secret. I knew your life would never be blank or grey, with boredom stretching out in front of you as far as you could see like some bad joke. I mean, I had everything, right? Why couldn't I be happy?'

Her heart thumped so loud she was sure he could hear it.

'So I decided I would watch you, get to know you, so I could discover where your relish for life came from and why it was you saw everything in brighter colours than I did.'

'Did you find an answer?'

'It was one of my epiphanies.'

'And?' She blinked. What was her secret?

'Love,' he said softly. 'You're not afraid to love. You care about so many different things and it gives you joy and enthusiasm and life.'

Except when he'd walked away from her after she'd told him she loved him. That blankness he'd described had descended on her then.

'And it hit me that I've spent my entire life trying not to care about things because you never know when they might be taken away—trying not to care about people because you never knew when they'd let you down.'

She reached out to lay a hand against his cheek. 'Oh,

Dominic,' she whispered. He'd lost so much. She didn't blame him for protecting his heart.

'I don't want to live like that any more, Bella. Since I've met you I haven't had a single dull moment. A lot of frustrating ones, perhaps, but no dull ones. You make my life so much brighter, clearer, better. I love you. I never knew I could love someone so…hard. So please, Bella, will you marry me? Will you build a life with me? Will you be mine for ever?'

She pulled her hand from his face and clutched it in her lap. Her heart thumped so hard that for a moment she couldn't speak. 'Dominic, if I walked away from you now, what would you do?'

His face twisted. His pain wrapped about her and she almost relented, but she needed to know his answer. More importantly, she suspected that he needed to know the answer.

He sat back on his heels. 'I wouldn't blame you for it, Bella. I've treated you shockingly.' His eyes suddenly flamed. 'But I will not do what my father did! I will not fall apart. He thought he could only find strength and meaning in his relationships with women. You've shown me that's not true. I will keep working hard. I will develop friendships with people I like. I will find hobbies I enjoy and immerse myself in those.' He stilled and swallowed. 'Are you going to walk away, Bella?'

Not a chance! She shifted until she was kneeling in front of him. 'Are you sure you know what you're letting yourself in for? I'll want a dog.'

'We'll get two.'

'I want a house in the suburbs.'

'A big one,' he agreed, 'that we can fill with children. And not too far from Marco, so he can visit whenever he wants.'

Her heart threatened to beat a path clean out of her chest. 'I don't want a husband who spends two or three months at a time away from home.'

'I'm not leaving you for two or three days, let alone two or three months.' He shook his head emphatically. 'We're going to build that dream restaurant of yours. You and me.'

They were? Her heart started to soar.

'You cook the best food I have ever eaten in my life but you couldn't design a realistic business-plan to save your life—you'd blow the budget. That's where you need me. I'll keep you on budget. Plus I can play host whenever you need me to. Plus someone will need to look after the children when you're busy.'

She took his face in her hands. 'Dominic, I want you to be happy. You don't have to want all those things, too. I will take you any way you come. We can compromise and—'

'I don't want to compromise, Bella. Those are the things I want. That's the life I want. With you.'

She wondered if she had stars in her eyes because his face grew soft. 'Dominic,' she whispered. 'Most of all I just want you. Yes, I would love to marry you. Nothing could make me happier.'

He grinned. It was slow in coming, but when it did it was low and wide and it made her pulse jump. 'You said yes.' His smile grew kind of goofy. 'You said yes,' he repeated.

She found herself starting to laugh. 'This is the part where you're supposed to kiss me.'

He wrapped an arm about her waist and pulled her flush up against him. His free hand tipped her chin up before caressing the skin of her throat. The goofiness vanished and pure wickedness replaced it. 'Your every wish,' he murmured against her lips, before he captured them in a kiss that Bella prayed would never end.

* * * * *

Mills & Boon® Hardback

September 2012

ROMANCE

Unlocking her Innocence	Lynne Graham
Santiago's Command	Kim Lawrence
His Reputation Precedes Him	Carole Mortimer
The Price of Retribution	Sara Craven
Just One Last Night	Helen Brooks
The Greek's Acquisition	Chantelle Shaw
The Husband She Never Knew	Kate Hewitt
When Only Diamonds Will Do	Lindsay Armstrong
The Couple Behind the Headlines	Lucy King
The Best Mistake of Her Life	Aimee Carson
The Valtieri Baby	Caroline Anderson
Slow Dance with the Sheriff	Nikki Logan
Bella's Impossible Boss	Michelle Douglas
The Tycoon's Secret Daughter	Susan Meier
She's So Over Him	Joss Wood
Return of the Last McKenna	Shirley Jump
Once a Playboy...	Kate Hardy
Challenging the Nurse's Rules	Janice Lynn

MEDICAL

Her Motherhood Wish	Anne Fraser
A Bond Between Strangers	Scarlet Wilson
The Sheikh and the Surrogate Mum	Meredith Webber
Tamed by her Brooding Boss	Joanna Neil

Mills & Boon® Large Print

September 2012

ROMANCE

A Vow of Obligation	Lynne Graham
Defying Drakon	Carole Mortimer
Playing the Greek's Game	Sharon Kendrick
One Night in Paradise	Maisey Yates
Valtieri's Bride	Caroline Anderson
The Nanny Who Kissed Her Boss	Barbara McMahon
Falling for Mr Mysterious	Barbara Hannay
The Last Woman He'd Ever Date	Liz Fielding
His Majesty's Mistake	Jane Porter
Duty and the Beast	Trish Morey
The Darkest of Secrets	Kate Hewitt

HISTORICAL

Lady Priscilla's Shameful Secret	Christine Merrill
Rake with a Frozen Heart	Marguerite Kaye
Miss Cameron's Fall from Grace	Helen Dickson
Society's Most Scandalous Rake	Isabelle Goddard
The Taming of the Rogue	Amanda McCabe

MEDICAL

Falling for the Sheikh She Shouldn't	Fiona McArthur
Dr Cinderella's Midnight Fling	Kate Hardy
Brought Together by Baby	Margaret McDonagh
One Month to Become a Mum	Louisa George
Sydney Harbour Hospital: Luca's Bad Girl	Amy Andrews
The Firebrand Who Unlocked His Heart	Anne Fraser

Mills & Boon® Hardback

October 2012

ROMANCE

Banished to the Harem	Carol Marinelli
Not Just the Greek's Wife	Lucy Monroe
A Delicious Deception	Elizabeth Power
Painted the Other Woman	Julia James
A Game of Vows	Maisey Yates
A Devil in Disguise	Caitlin Crews
Revelations of the Night Before	Lynn Raye Harris
Defying her Desert Duty	Annie West
The Wedding Must Go On	Robyn Grady
The Devil and the Deep	Amy Andrews
Taming the Brooding Cattleman	Marion Lennox
The Rancher's Unexpected Family	Myrna Mackenzie
Single Dad's Holiday Wedding	Patricia Thayer
Nanny for the Millionaire's Twins	Susan Meier
Truth-Or-Date.com	Nina Harrington
Wedding Date with Mr Wrong	Nicola Marsh
The Family Who Made Him Whole	Jennifer Taylor
The Doctor Meets Her Match	Annie Claydon

MEDICAL

A Socialite's Christmas Wish	Lucy Clark
Redeeming Dr Riccardi	Leah Martyn
The Doctor's Lost-and-Found Heart	Dianne Drake
The Man Who Wouldn't Marry	Tina Beckett

0912 GEN STD HB

Mills & Boon® Large Print

October 2012

ROMANCE

A Secret Disgrace	Penny Jordan
The Dark Side of Desire	Julia James
The Forbidden Ferrara	Sarah Morgan
The Truth Behind his Touch	Cathy Williams
Plain Jane in the Spotlight	Lucy Gordon
Battle for the Soldier's Heart	Cara Colter
The Navy SEAL's Bride	Soraya Lane
My Greek Island Fling	Nina Harrington
Enemies at the Altar	Melanie Milburne
In the Italian's Sights	Helen Brooks
In Defiance of Duty	Caitlin Crews

HISTORICAL

The Duchess Hunt	Elizabeth Beacon
Marriage of Mercy	Carla Kelly
Unbuttoning Miss Hardwick	Deb Marlowe
Chained to the Barbarian	Carol Townend
My Fair Concubine	Jeannie Lin

MEDICAL

Georgie's Big Greek Wedding?	Emily Forbes
The Nurse's Not-So-Secret Scandal	Wendy S. Marcus
Dr Right All Along	Joanna Neil
Summer With A French Surgeon	Margaret Barker
Sydney Harbour Hospital: Tom's Redemption	Fiona Lowe
Doctor on Her Doorstep	Annie Claydon

0912 GEN STD LP